Bromhead wondered why he found her attractive

Her whole attitude had been formed in a dreamworld, one that didn't exist, but it was impossible to convince her of that. "Your kind always turn to personal insults when they have no argument."

"My kind?" She looked puzzled.

"You pinko university liberals."

Now she smiled. "You see? True to form. Even down to the clichés used by the military."

"Then why aren't the university types in the streets over the North Vietnamese atrocities? They propose holiday cease-fires, then break them at will. The Communists violate the neutrality of Laos and Cambodia and no one cares. Hell, there are even advisers from Red China in South Vietnam and no one cares."

"That's different," said Jane Lucas.

"How in hell is it different?"

She paused before speaking again. "I knew it would do no good coming here. I thought I could reason with you, but I was wrong. I hope you don't get too many of these people killed." She moved rapidly to the door.

Bromhead called after her. "I hope you don't get them *all* killed."

VIETNAM: GROUND ZERO ™

THE VILLE

ERIC HELM

A GOLD EAGLE BOOK FROM
WORLDWIDE ®

TORONTO • NEW YORK • LONDON • PARIS
AMSTERDAM • STOCKHOLM • HAMBURG
ATHENS • MILAN • TOKYO • SYDNEY

First edition December 1987

ISBN 0-373-62709-2

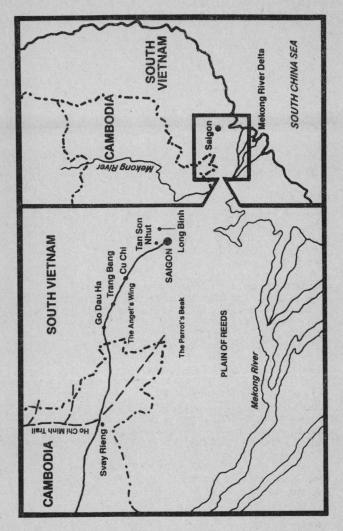

VIETNAM: GROUND ZERO ™

THE VILLE

PROLOGUE

FRENCH INDOCHINA, 1954

A short, coded radio message had come in the middle of the night. The brief transmission had been tinged with panic: a single, almost frantic order to pull out and take everything of French manufacture or design that was stored in the village.

As soon as he had received the message, Jacques Zouave switched off his radio and left the hut. It was a dilapidated thatched structure that kept out the monsoon rains but not the humidity of the jungle. A notched log, which served as stairs, led from the door to the muddy ground three feet below. The hootch was set up on stubby stilts to keep out the water and to discourage the night creatures.

Now, Zouave dropped silently to the ground, then glanced toward the edge of the jungle that loomed in the dark like the gates to a mystical forest. He knew that a guard was supposed to be watching the trails that led to the village. Zouave turned to his left and worked his way uphill, his feet slipping on the wet ground. Once, he had to put out a hand to steady himself, his fingers brushing the mud, which he wiped on the ragged black cotton shirt he wore.

He approached the hootch where his commander slept. It was a carbon copy of his own. Thatched roof and walls that rose from a platform of logs lashed together to make a rough, splinter-studded floor. Zouave stopped by the door, an opening in the thatch with no covering, and whispered at the interior, "Sir, I have a message."

A moment later Michel Sahraoui appeared in the doorway, his face pale against the darkness of the interior. "What is it?" he asked.

"We are ordered to leave here. Tonight, if possible. Tomorrow at the latest."

Sahraoui got up from his sleeping pallet of woven bamboo and nimbly made his way down the notched log to stand barefoot in the mud. "Let me see the message."

"I destroyed it as soon as I decoded it."

"Ah. And were we given a reason for this sudden order?"

"No, sir. Just that we are to collect all our equipment, move to the landing strip and wait for evacuation by noon tomorrow. We are to leave with as little fanfare as possible, making certain that nothing French remains behind."

Sahraoui pushed a hand through his disheveled dark hair and stared into the night. "You are sure of the message?"

"Yes, sir. It was repeated twice and I copied it down twice and checked both versions."

"All right, then. Let's wake the others, check the weapons inventory and the equipment hootches. Let's do it as quickly and quietly as possible."

Zouave turned and disappeared into the darkness, heading back toward his hut and his radio. Sahraoui placed one foot on the notched log, careful not to slip, and crouched as he stepped through the low doorway. Then he dropped on all fours so that he could crawl to his sleeping mat. He reached out and touched the bare shoulder of the woman who had not stirred when Zouave delivered the message.

Sahraoui sat and crossed his legs, staring at the darker outline of the figure in the gloom. She belonged to the Meo tribe, a light-skinned race found throughout Indochina. Her long black hair reflected the starlight that invaded the hootch. She was an attractive woman whose features indicated that she might have had French in her ancestry. She spoke French fluently and had begun as their interpretor, evolving into something more, at least to Sahraoui.

"Are you awake?" he asked.

She rolled to her back and then turned her head so that she could look at him. "Yes." There was a glistening on her cheek, just under her eyes.

"Then you have heard?"

"Yes."

Sahraoui sat for a moment watching her, waiting for her to give him a clue to her reaction, but she didn't move or speak. He glanced away from her, at the uniform that was folded and sitting on the crude wooden chair. He had constructed it from teak and bamboo because he occasionally felt the need to sit in one. There were other things, a cabinet that held a cooking pot and eating utensils, clay pots and even a small mirror, on the other side of the hootch. Next to it were Sahraoui's rifle and ammunition, his rucksack and a box of grenades stenciled U.S. Army.

When he looked at the woman again, she had sat up facing him. Her bare breasts were visible in the dim light. He reached out as if to touch her and then drew his hand back.

"What will happen to you?" he asked.

"I will live here and someday a warrior who wants children will come into my house."

Sahraoui stood and moved to his uniform. It had been a while since he had needed to wear it. Training and advising the Meos had dictated he wear the same as they. He had grown used to the loosely wrapped loincloth. As he struggled into the uniform, he found it constricting, unpleasant to wear. It was almost impossible to pull on the boots. His feet had changed during the months of barefoot activity.

As he finished dressing, he turned to see her studying him. He knelt and took one of her hands. "You could come with us. You speak their language and ours and that is a valuable asset." He tried to ignore the tears that were now obvious on her face, pretending they weren't there.

"No, I think not. My people are here."

A whisper from outside called him. He dropped her hand and picked up his weapon. "I have work to do. I shall come back before we depart."

She grabbed his arm and pulled him toward her, brushing his lips lightly with her own. "Do not forget me."

He sighed. "I could never do that." He tasted the salt of her tears and found he could ignore that, too.

BY EIGHT, THEY HAD STRIPPED the arms locker of all the weapons, moving not only the rifles and pistols, but also the machine guns, mortars and recoilless rifles. They had stacked the crates of ammunition near the weapons, and then toured the perimeter of the village, collecting the arms they had emplaced in the bunkers.

Now that all the weapons had been accounted for, they began picking up the radio equipment, the entrenching tools, rucksacks and the knives. They required the men to turn in their boots, uniforms and even their underwear. Everything that looked like it was of French manufacture was taken and piled at the grass-covered airstrip.

All morning Sahraoui had been turning away his friends. They had come to trust him and the other French paratroopers, but were now to be stripped of all means of protecting themselves. He refused each request for a rifle or pistol or grenade. He told each of them that he was sorry, but he had his orders and they all knew what that meant. Each time he gave the speech, he felt that he was betraying a friend. To make it worse, none of them protested or argued the refusal.

At ten, Sahraoui stood among the crates and equipment, counting softly to himself, feeling miserable. His uniform was soaked with sweat and it was like wearing a wet towel in a steam bath. Sunlight streamed through the gaps in the trees near the airstrip, making it so hot that nearly everyone refused to walk out to the airfield where there was no protection from the sun.

After he finished counting, Sahraoui sat on one of the wooden crates, pulled a cloth from his pocket and mopped his face. As his gaze found the village a hundred yards away near the crest of a hill, he saw a column of smoke mushroom toward the sky. A moment later there was a flat bang that set the monkeys scurrying and the birds flying.

Sahraoui leaped off the crate and snatched his rifle. Behind him, his men were spreading out, their weapons ready as firing erupted in the village. Over the staccato reports of gunfire, there were shouts and screams of pain and anguish. The people fled the village, running into the jungle or toward the landing strip.

The timing of the Viet Minh assault was perfect. With no weapons left in the village, the residents couldn't retaliate. The discipline they had learned from the French disintegrated under the onslaught. Without their weapons, they felt vulnerable, and ran in panic.

There were more explosions as the Viet Minh grenaded the hootches, shooting as they found human targets. Crouched behind the protection of their crates, their weapons held at the ready, the Frenchmen saw the villagers appear, running at them. The firing at the edge of the village increased then. Sahraoui saw a man lifted off his feet, his chest blossoming crimson as he fell among the trees. A bullet hit a woman in the middle of the back, snapping her spine and exiting between her breasts. She collapsed in a loose-boned heap, dead before she hit the ground. Two men were cut down by machine gun fire that ripped through their stomachs.

Sahraoui recognized his Meo wife running through the jungle, her bare breasts bouncing. He raised a hand to wave, as if beckoning her. Her face was a mask of fear, her eyes wide, her mouth open but no sound coming from it. Once, she glanced over her shoulder and stumbled, by stayed on her feet.

A bullet struck her in the shoulder then, slamming her to the ground. She started to rise, her face and chest a mass of scratches, blood and mud. She uttered a cry of agony as the pain from the wound coursed through her. The sound propelled Sahraoui into action, and he was up and running as she fell back to the soft wet earth, disappearing in the short grass.

And then the Viet Minh were shooting at him, their bullets buzzing the air near him like angry bees. He dived for cover, his hands over his head as the odor of the hot, damp earth overwhelmed him.

Sahraoui's men opened fire, first with their rifles, then with one of the machine guns, halting the Viet Minh advance at the edge of the village. The enemy leaped for cover as the hammering of the .30 caliber slammed into the trees and bushes and ground around them.

The villagers were nowhere in sight. Sahraoui guessed that they were either dead or wounded in the village, or running through the jungle searching for places to hide.

The Viet Minh lost interest in them, turning their attention to the French soldiers. Suddenly the enemy attacked, materializing out of the jungle, firing and shouting as they came. But they ran into a fierce barrage of return fire from the paratroopers that stopped them immediately.

When there was a lull in the firing, Sahraoui crawled to his men who were still crouched among the boxes and crates. He rose to his knees and aimed at the trees, but saw no targets.

"Michel, we have to get out of here," said Zouave.

Sahraoui noted the position of the sun above the airfield, then looked at his watch. It would be more than an hour before the plane arrived, if it ever did. Above the trees he could see a dense cloud of black smoke that showed where the village was burning fiercely.

"Can't leave all this equipment," he said.

"Then burn it. Use the white phosphorus grenades to set it on fire. Then we get out."

"No," said Sahraoui, shaking his head. "We stay."

Then, to the left, more firing broke out. Rifle and machine gun bullets raked their position, kicking up clouds of dirt and splintering the wood of the boxes. Sahraoui dived out of the way and came up firing, emptying his weapon at the enemy who were hidden by the thick green vegetation.

"All right," he said. "Let's get out. Zouave, Grauwin and Mordal, grab the grenades and set them. Pull the pins and place them under the boxes so that they won't arm themselves until the boxes are moved. The rest of you each grab two of the grenades."

The three men worked feverishly to place the booby traps under the crates and weapons. When they finished they grabbed their rifles but kept their heads down as the Viet Minh continued to snipe.

"Fall back," ordered Sahraoui. "Fall back."

Some of the men ran from their cover near the boxes, heading for the jungle and better protection. The others turned their weapons on the Viet Minh positions, firing as fast as they could, forcing the enemy to keep their heads down.

Sahraoui kept glancing at the spot where he had seen his wife struck down. There had been no sign of her since; he was now convinced that she was dead.

Suddenly, rounds slamming into the crate near his head diverted his attention. Muzzle-flashes winked in the dense vegetation where the sun couldn't wash it out. He aimed at the center of it, triggered his weapon twice and waited. Whoever was shooting at him didn't return fire.

By this time his men had reached the edge of the jungle on the other side of the airfield and opened fire to protect the rest of the units. Almost as one, although Sahraoui gave no command, the men were up and running.

One of Sahraoui's men grunted with pain and fell. His head hung down and his weapon was near his hand. Sahraoui slid to a stop and turned. He came back and reached out as a second round hit the man with a loud wet slap. As he fell forward, he looked up at Sahraoui but said nothing. His eyes seemed to roll up in his head and he dropped forward into a spreading pool of red.

Sahraoui spun and ran for the jungle. Even the short sprint sucked the breath from his lungs and covered his face with sweat. He felt an adrenaline rush, which created a nervous tension. He could almost imagine the impact of a slug slamming into the base of his spine. At the tree line, he dived over a log, rolled, and came up on a knee in a puddle of muck that quickly soaked through his uniform. The trees and bushes around him shuddered as Viet Minh bullets whistled through them. Shredded leaves, bits of bark, and splinters rained down around him.

Over his shoulder, he spotted a lone Viet Minh soldier. The man wore an OD uniform and carried an old rifle, poking the barrel into the bushes. Sahraoui leaned to the right, supporting himself on his elbow. He let the sights search for the enemy and when the man stepped into the sight picture, Sahraoui squeezed the trigger. The soldier jerked once, reached up to where the blood was pouring from his throat and began to fall. He reached out with one hand as if to break the fall, then disappeared.

As soon as Sahraoui was clear, the men began throwing their grenades. The gray, tin-can-like bombs arced toward the crates of rifles, ammunition and supplies, and detonated into glowing clouds of burning white. The flaming debris rained down, setting everything near them on fire. Smoke from the damp green vegetation billowed upward, obscuring the landing strip and the jungle beyond it.

When it was obvious that the equipment was burning ferociously, Sahraoui ordered, "Let's get out of here. It's time to get out."

"What about the airplane?"

"They'll never land when they see all the smoke. They'll divert and try to raise us on the radio."

"Where will we be?"

Sahraoui pointed. "Escaping through the jungle."

The men turned, with Mordal running ahead to take the point. As he disappeared into the jungle, Sahraoui took a final look behind him. He could not see the village, although black smoke still marked its location. There were no villagers about. He figured that the survivors were scattered through the jungle. All he could see were the flames from the burning equipment. Then the ammo began to cook off. The detonating rounds, some of them tracers, flashed randomly into the jungle or skyward with streaks of red. Sahraoui decided that it was time to escape.

FOUR WEEKS LATER, the remnants of his unit were picked up by a patrol boat scouting the Mekong River in Cambodia, and taken to Saigon. They were put on a plane for France. None would return to Vietnam or Laos, even after the United States entered the war. Sahraoui never did find out what happened to his Meo wife, although he would think of her often. But for him, the war in Indochina was over.

1

MACV HEADQUARTERS, SAIGON, RVN

Army Captain Jonathan Bromhead, a tall, freckle-faced kid who had completed one tour in Vietnam and was well into a second, sat in the air-conditioned conference room, sipping Coke from a can and waiting for the briefing to start. The room was small, just big enough for the mahogany table that was surrounded by eight low-backed, cloth-covered chairs. Stuck in one corner, crowding the table, was a screen and opposite it, near the door was a small table holding a Kodak carousel slide projector. On the walls, which had been paneled with pressed wood that imitated teak, were a number of framed prints showing the U.S. Army in battle.

The door opened and a Marine sergeant, dressed in jungle fatigues and spit-shined boots, entered the room. The Marine was a big man with no visible neck. Although he had shaved that morning, his cheeks were blue-black with stubble, and thick eyebrows met over his nose. He had light-colored eyes and his head had been shaved. There were sweat stains under his arms, down the front of his shirt and around his waist, where his pistol belt had been.

"You Bromhead?" asked the Marine.

"Captain Bromhead, yes."

"Sorry, sir. I'm Staff Sergeant Nicholas Gilman. I was told to report to you in here."

Bromhead stood and realized that the Marine was two or three inches taller than he was, and at six-one, Bromhead wasn't considered short. He stuck out his hand. "You were told to report to me?"

"Yes, sir."

"Did they say what it was about?"

"No, sir. Just said to find you in here and wait with you."

Bromhead picked up his Coke and drained it, then set the can on the table. "Well, this beats walking around in the jungle."

The door opened again and another sergeant entered. Directly behind him was an Army lieutenant colonel carrying a thick stack of folders. He kicked the door shut with his heel, dropped the files on the table and then switched on the slide projector.

"Okay," he said, "I'm Colonel Petersen and will be working as your liaison officer here. This other gentleman is Sergeant David Hansen."

Hansen was smaller than Gilman and Bromhead. He was just under six feet tall with a slight build. His jungle fatigues were brand new as were his boots. There was no evidence that he had been outside in the past week. His face was neither tanned nor sunburned and he looked like a clerk who had escaped from the boring duty of typing morning reports and duty rosters. He sat on the opposite side of the table and said nothing to anyone.

Petersen opened one of the folders, took out a number of aerial photographs and gave one each to Bromhead, Gilman and Hansen.

"This small village is anti-Communist," Petersen began. "It's inhabited by an ethnic group known as the Meo. They've lived in the region for hundreds of years and are familiar with everything that goes on in it.''

Petersen moved to the slide projector and picked up the remote control. He flashed through several of the slides that showed a village made of thatched hootches on stilts. Some of the scenes depicted people dressed in very little gathered around a cooking fire. Men chopping the heads off monkeys, a woman stirring a large black pot and children running wild.

''Okay,'' he said when he stopped. ''That shows the natives at home and at work. From this point on, anything I say in this room is classified as secret. Is that understood?''

Bromhead nodded and in unison the sergeants replied, ''Yes, sir.''

Petersen hit the remote control and a map of Southeast Asia appeared. He moved to the screen and picked up a pointer. ''The village we saw is located right here in Laos. It is no more than ten or twelve klicks from a main trunk of the Ho Chi Minh Trail north and east of Ban Tasseing.''

He let the words sink in and then snapped off the projector lamp, leaving the fan motor running. Taking a seat at the head of the table, he opened the top folder. ''Now, what we have determined, studying the old records from the French paras, is that the men of the village have received some military instruction. There are approximately seventy military-age males available there, and another two hundred and eighty in villages no more than seven klicks away.''

The colonel studied each man's face in turn. ''Since the name of the game is going to be Vietnamization, or in this case Laoization, we're going to put a team into the area to raise a strike battalion with an eye on interdicting the traffic on the Ho Chi Minh Trail. By the way, this plan for Vietnamization is not yet a matter of public record, so let's keep it under our hats.''

Bromhead glanced at the men with him. A Marine NCO and an Air Force sergeant. He twisted the aerial photo around and stared at it. It was little more than a black and white map of the area.

"Handled properly, this could slow the traffic on the Trail to a trickle and relieve a number of units of their duty on the border in South Vietnam."

"Isn't this a MACV-SOG project? I mean, isn't this the kind of thing they're trained to do?"

"You're right there," Petersen replied. "But with the new demands on people with a Special Forces background for a wide variety of missions, the Special Forces are strapped to complete the missions they already have. Captain Bromhead, you've already been in the area and worked with a number of the locals. That puts you one up on most of the people. Sergeant Gilman was unfortunate enough to go to the Marine Corps language school and is conversant in the Meo dialect. Since we wanted to keep the nature of the mission as integrated as possible, meaning we wanted someone from the Air Force involved, too, we recruited Sergeant Hansen. His own specialty is in organizing and training local populations in guerrilla warfare as it relates to airfield defense. Also, he has an expert knowledge of the radio and a fluency in French."

"Where?" asked Bromhead.

"If you're worried about me," said Hansen, his voice high and squeaky, "I've worked with the British SAS in Malaysia and with the Special Forces in both Cambodia and South Vietnam."

"No," said Bromhead. "I just wondered where you've been training those people."

"It's a program that's just getting under way."

"Uh-huh," said Bromhead.

"These people, these Meos, they know we're coming?" asked Gilman.

Petersen waded through the folder as if looking for the answer to the question. "Given the high concentration of enemy soldiers in the area, we thought it best to go in cold—"

"Colonel Petersen," interrupted Bromhead. "Why not let me put this together with my team. I've a couple of good men with real experience in this . . ."

"But they aren't conversant in the native language."

"No, sir, they aren't, but I know of a Nung tribesman who can speak that language and English. Sergeant Krung could handle the translating duties."

"I'm sorry." Petersen shook his head. "But the team has already been determined and their backgrounds have already been checked."

"My men all have the appropriate clearances."

"What about this Sergeant Krung? I trust his background hasn't been checked to the same degree."

"Maybe not, but I trust him and in the end, it's my life that's on the line."

Petersen made a show of considering Bromhead's proposal and then shook his head. "No. This is set up for now. No time to change."

"I can have my men ready to go in the morning," insisted Bromhead.

"I'm sorry, Captain, but we've already stripped too many of the A Detachments. I don't want to take any more men out of the camps if I can help it. We have trained people available, we have them in place and I think we'll go with the team we have assembled here."

Bromhead was going to press further, but then realized that Petersen's next move would be to make it an order, stopping all debate. There was no sense going to that extreme now, since it would do no good.

Changing the direction of the conversation again, Bromhead said, "How do we know these people will support us?"

"Oh, don't worry about that," said Petersen. "The Vietcong have been working that area for years. The Viet Minh before that. Their demands for taxes and their forced recruitment of the young men and women have not endeared them. Besides, there's a traditional animosity between the Meos and the lowland Vietnamese. Hell, the Vietnamese have persecuted these people for centuries. Give them an excuse to kill Vietnamese, they'll take it."

Bromhead shook his head. "That still hasn't answered the question. How do we know that these people will support us?"

"I'm not at liberty to discuss all the details of the preliminary recon. Suffice it to say that the question was asked at the proper time and in the proper place. The people there will support us."

"When was the last time anyone was there?" asked Gilman. "And what equipment do the natives have?"

"The recent recons suggest that they have nothing other than a few primitive firearms and their homemade weapons."

Bromhead shook his head. "This just isn't going to work. It'd take weeks, if not months, to put together a fighting force out of the tribesmen. We don't have that kind of time."

"You'll have all the time you need," said Petersen. "Once you're established in the village, you can proceed with the training at your own pace. You'll be on your own to establish your schedule."

"Colonel, I have a camp of my own. There are things there that have to be done. I can't be running all over Southeast Asia."

Petersen closed his folder and folded his hands. "You have an executive officer there, Lieutenant Mildebrandt. Isn't he capable of running the camp in your absence?"

"Of course," said Bromhead. "He'll do an excellent job, but it's not his to do. It's mine."

"Then consider this mission to be your new job for the time being." Petersen's face was impassive. "Unless you've misled me about Lieutenant Mildebrandt's ability. If that's the case, I can get someone else in there."

Bromhead realized that he had been outmaneuvered again. He fell silent.

"We'll need equipment and supplies," said Hansen, filling the silence. "I don't see any airfields around there."

"Initial insertion will be by helicopter. You'll take in just enough to get started. Some weapons so that you can mount the guard and organize the first-strike companies. You'll want to get an airstrip established that will take an Otter."

"Jesus," said Gilman.

"The Special Forces do this all the time. It's an offshoot of the strategic hamlet concept. We just want to expand it outward, cover more ground."

Petersen then went on to explain the plan a second time. Each man had been selected because of his background so that no special training was needed. All they had to do were the jobs they had been trained to do. It was just one more assignment for them. Contact would be maintained and if the situation warranted it, they could be pulled out.

"Your only instruction is not to get captured. Although you'll be working for our government, you won't be wearing any U.S. insignia and all the weapons will be sterile. This will be a covert operation."

"Do we have a choice in the matter?" asked Gilman.

"Certainly, Sergeant. You're free to refuse the mission, remembering, of course, that your refusal will be noted in your 201 File." Petersen flashed a grin, devoid of mirth.

"When do we start?" Bromhead's shoulders drooped resignedly.

"Airlift will be available tomorrow afternoon. Insertion will be just before dawn the following day. You'll be responsible for making contact with the villagers and enlisting their aid. Anything else?''

''Neither of the men here has been described as a medic. You have one assigned?''

''This is a covert mission and we don't want to drop a lot of people into it who aren't needed.''

''Excuse me, Colonel,'' said Bromhead, ''but a medic is not someone who only adds to the complexity of the mission. He is an essential part of it. The Special Forces doesn't send a team out without one. Hell, sir, we've gone out with surgeons.''

''There isn't a medic available.''

''I can rustle one up quickly. It won't be a problem.''

Petersen made a show of searching through his file folders. ''I'll make the arrangements for a medic. I've a couple of names here. I'll have one of them meet us at Bien Hoa in the morning. Okay?''

''That'll be fine, Colonel,'' said Bromhead.

Petersen's gaze rested on each man. ''Now, are there any other questions before we adjourn?''

A hundred additional questions sprang to mind, but all Bromhead said was, ''We'll need maps to get into the area. And the equipment.''

''All being arranged. You'll have a final briefing tomorrow just before you take off. Report back here at noon.'' Petersen shook his head. ''We were going to hold you incommunicado but decided that it wasn't necessary. Don't talk about this to anyone. Until tomorrow at noon, you're free to do what you want. Buy a steak, drink, but be ready on time.''

BROMHEAD SPENT THE FIRST PART of the afternoon alone and then headed over to the Carasel Hotel hoping to find either Gerber or Fetterman or with luck, both. He walked through the lobby, a cavernous structure containing a dozen chairs, a half dozen couches and numerous tables that looked as if they had been stolen over several decades and from different parts of the world.

He exited, passing through French doors and out onto the open-air bar. For a moment he stood there, surveying the crowd. There were civilians, most of them working for the various media or at the embassy, and a scattering of military types in jungle fatigues and khakis. Bright sunlight hid some of them. Bromhead heard a laugh that sounded like breaking crystal. He recognized the voice immediately.

He glanced to the rear of the bar, saw Fetterman, Gerber, and finally Robin Morrow. He shouldered his way between two male reporters, one of them wearing a safari jacket. Bromhead reached the table and grabbed a vacant chair without waiting for an invitation.

As he dropped into it, Anthony Fetterman, a small, wiry man with balding, wavy black hair and dark, almost olive complexion, glanced at him. On his first tour, Fetterman had been the team sergeant of the A Detachment where Bromhead worked. "Johnnie. It's good to see you."

Mack Gerber, a tall, thin officer with brown hair and blue eyes, held a hand across the table. He was the detachment commander. "Good to see you." He then turned to Fetterman. "Calls himself Jack now instead of Johnnie."

Robin Morrow turned so that she was facing him. Her long, brown hair was cut with bangs that brushed her green eyes. She smiled at him, the perspiration from the humidity beading on her lip. "Jack, huh? I like that."

"Thought it was better for the team leader to be known as Jack."

"So, Johnnie, ah, Jack, can I interest you in a drink?"

"Of course, Captain. I'm always in the mood for a drink."

Gerber beckoned the waitress, a Vietnamese woman in a skimpy costume that didn't seem to keep her cool. He ordered a round. Robin leaned on the table, cupping her chin in one hand. "What brings you to Saigon?"

Bromhead glanced furtively right and left before answering, more concerned about Morrow than Gerber and Fetterman. Morrow, as a journalist, was always looking for a story and his later mission would make a great one. "That's a question I can't answer. High-level briefing and then I'm off again."

"Uh-huh," said Fetterman. He grinned and added, "You sound like you just escaped from a second-rate spy thriller. High-level briefing."

"It's true," protested Bromhead, and then laughed as he realized Fetterman was baiting him.

"You can tell your old friendly sergeant," said Fetterman. "I know all anyway."

Bromhead shot another glance at Morrow but said nothing. He was saved when the drinks arrived.

Gerber picked up the ball then and said, "You here for a while or you heading back to your camp?"

"I'm here overnight and then off in the morning for a briefing. I won't be at the camp for a while." As he said it, he wondered if he was giving too much away, especially in front of Morrow, but decided that he had to say something. Either Gerber or Fetterman could make a single inquiry and find out that he wasn't at the camp.

"So you'll be going into the field." Morrow was still trying to pump him for information.

Gerber caught the pained look on Bromhead's face. He knew the young captain didn't want to lie to Morrow so he jumped in again. "Robin, you have plans for dinner tonight or are you heading back to the office?"

"You offering to buy me dinner, Mack, or are you just trying to divert my attention?" She grinned at him.

"I didn't think I was that transparent. Of course I'm trying to divert the conversation, but if I have to buy you dinner to do it, then consider it done."

"And during dinner I can't ask about Johnnie's, rather, Jack's, mission?"

"Of course you can, but he gets to lie about it. He can make up all kinds of strange stories and you have to believe them, at least for tonight."

"I find your ground rules for the free dinner acceptable." Morrow laughed, showing perfect teeth. She liked the company of these men.

Gerber glanced at his watch. It was not the cheap, camouflage-covered one that he normally wore, but an expensive Seiko with the Special Forces crest engraved in the face. "I make it about seventeen hundred. An hour to get cleaned up and then meet in the lobby. From there we can decide where to go for dinner."

Morrow slid her chair back and stood. "I'll go to the room first and get changed. You can meet me there in a few minutes."

"Fine."

She turned and made her way through the crowd, each of the men at the table watching her retreat, the hem of her short skirt dancing around her shapely legs. They could see the perspiration dampening her blouse down the back so that the material was nearly invisible and the thin line of her bra showed through plainly.

When she disappeared, Bromhead turned to Gerber. "She staying in the hotel?"

Gerber didn't respond, but Fetterman did. He smiled evilly. "Our captain has himself a roommate."

"Oh?" said Bromhead. "What about Karen?"

Again it was Fetterman who answered. "I think Karen cut her own throat with our captain."

"If you two are through discussing my sex life and relation-ships, I think we could move on to more important things, like dinner." He reached into his pocket for a handful of change.

"We should take Jack out and get him drunk," said Fet-terman.

"A good plan." Gerber dropped his coins on the table, saw that one of them wasn't money, but a silver-dollar-sized token with the Trojan Horse on it that he carried for luck. He picked it up and slipped it into his pocket. "Any place you want to go?"

"Just where they have loud music, beer, and women danc-ing."

Fetterman said, "Then it's decided. I know just the place. Shall we adjourn?"

THEY SPENT THE EVENING in various clubs drinking beer with Bromhead chasing women, none of whom he caught. At one point they ordered massive steak dinners with everything in-cluding the baked potato because they figured it would be a long time before Bromhead got the chance to eat that well again. By two they were tired and headed back to the BOQ at Tan Son Nhut to drop off Bromhead. He stood watching the lights of the jeep as they drove away.

The next morning slightly hung over, he got dressed and went to find breakfast. By noon he was back at the MACV Headquarters and waiting for his instructions. He was joined by Hansen and Gilman and three of them were given new uni-forms that contained no U.S. insignia, weapons that looked like leftovers from the Second World War and several duffel bags full of equipment that could not be directly traced to the United States.

After another briefing that provided little additional infor-mation, they were taken outside where a driver and a three-quarter-ton truck were waiting. Gilman and Hansen tossed the gear into the back and climbed in after it. Bromhead got into the front, on a seat that was dirty and torn, and nodded at the driver. Within minutes they were on the streets of Saigon, winding their way to the north and Bien Hoa where their transportation waited.

They bounced along crowded streets that were jammed with men in uniform and women in the traditional *ao dai*. Heavily made-up prostitutes lounged on some of the corners, their skirts no more than wide belts and their blouses either see-through or incredibly tight. Hundreds of Lambrettas swerved among the military vehicles and countless bicycles. The driver dodged through the traffic, missing the Hondas and pedestrians, finding the gaps in the traffic just before they closed.

Bromhead sat with his back braced against the door and one hand on the dashboard. He listened to the rumbling diesel engine and tried to ignore the stench of exhaust fumes. Once, when the driver swerved too close to a gaudily painted car, he found himself jamming his feet against the floorboards, but said nothing.

Soon they left the city and headed into open country that seemed to have been bulldozed. The green of the jungle had been stripped away to reveal the reddish brown earth. Water from the various rivers had spread from their banks, flooding some of the surrounding area and puddles winked brightly in afternoon sun. Men and women were working, along with machinery, some of it painted yellow and some of it OD green.

Across the river they turned to the west and entered the Bien Hoa military complex. The MP at the makeshift gate didn't even leave the guard hut. He waved an arm out the window, telling them to proceed.

The driver ground the gears as they rolled along a dirt road, kicking up a choking cloud of red dust. They left the built-up area and pulled into an open park that overlooked the edge of the airfield. A jeep sat to one side, next to a CH-47 Chinook with the ramp down and the doors open. The flight crew seemed to be lounging in the shade of the chopper, drinking Cokes from clear glass bottles.

As Bromhead got out of the truck, Petersen walked over. He jerked a thumb over his shoulder. "Gear is loaded on the chopper. Got a list in the jeep and you can sign for it."

Bromhead gave Petersen a strange look. He passed a hand over his face and wiped the sweat onto the front of his jungle fatigues. He took off the soft fatigue hat and mopped his forehead with his sleeve. Finally he said, "I don't sign for anything until I see all that I'm signing for. And I don't sign for anything that I'm expected to leave in the field."

"You have to sign for it," said Petersen.

"I don't have to do anything, Colonel," said Bromhead.

"Well, we won't worry about that right now. Why don't you have your men put their equipment in the chopper? You can check to see if you have everything you need."

Bromhead saw both Gilman and Hansen drop to the ground. They pulled their duffel bags from the rear of the truck. Gilman shouldered his and then grabbed Bromhead's.

"Thanks," said Bromhead.

"No sweat, sir."

Bromhead picked up his equipment and walked to the helicopter. He dropped the bag and moved toward the crewmen. "You all know exactly where we're going?"

The pilot was a young man with a permanently sunburned face, white-blond hair and almost nonexistent eyebrows. "We've been thoroughly briefed." He held a hand up to shade his eyes as he spoke.

"Then as soon as I've checked the gear and gotten my people on board, we'll be ready for takeoff."

The pilot stood, brushed the dirt off the seat of his uniform and said, "Right." He drained the Coke and handed the empty bottle to one of the others. "Let's do it."

As the crew scrambled to their positions, Bromhead and his men got their gear into the rear of the chopper. The crew chief took the duffel bags and stacked them in front of several crates that were lined up along the center of the aircraft. The crates were strapped to pallets that sat on rails, ball bearing-loaded metal strips that let one man push a huge load out of the helicopter. On each side of the fuselage were troop seats with a webbing of red that formed the backs of the seats.

Once everything was loaded, Bromhead stepped out and walked over to the jeep. Petersen was sitting in the passenger's side, his foot on the dash, gazing idly at the airfield around him. He turned and picked a clipboard off the rear seat when he saw Bromhead approaching.

Bromhead held out a palm. "I'm still not signing for anything."

"All the equipment there?"

"As near as I can tell, but I refuse to be responsible for something I can't carry out. We get into a bad situation and have to dump the equipment, I can see some rear-area bureaucrat tossing forms at me and deciding that I should pay for the stuff."

"That's not going to happen."

"Damn right," said Bromhead. "Anything else?"

"Hansen has the schedule for contacts. He knows how you're supposed to make any radio checks to prevent the enemy from triangulating. He has the codes for messages to you as well. He's been thoroughly briefed."

"Okay," said Bromhead. He glanced around. "I don't see the medic."

Petersen made a show of looking at his watch and then at his clipboard. "Guess he's not going to make it."

"You know, Colonel, I would be within my rights to refuse this mission right now. Special Forces will back me up all the way on this."

Petersen set his clipboard down and stared at the younger officer. "You will not scrap the mission because of this. You'll have one stop en route and if you can find a medic there who is qualified to work in the field, you take him. You cannot scrap the mission because the medic missed the flight."

For a moment Bromhead stood staring at the colonel. He didn't like going out without a medic, and there was still a chance that he could find one. He thought about it, almost refused and then decided that he would get one at the rest stop. He nodded. "Okay."

"Now, if it looks like the VC or NVA are going to make a push to overrun your camp, get out. You run into the night with Hansen and Gilman, and if you can't get out, make sure that neither of them is captured."

Bromhead stared directly into Petersen's eyes for a moment. "I assume you mean that as a last resort, I shoot them."

"That's right. Then you shoot yourself. It's the old Seventh Cavalry rule. Save the last round for yourself."

"Didn't do them a shit load of good, did it?"

"No, but those are your instructions."

"I don't suppose you'd want to give that to me in writing?"

"You suppose right."

Behind them there was a high-pitched whine as the turbine of one of the engines began to spin. The sound was followed by a roar as the engine reached operating rpm.

Petersen stuck his hand out. "Good luck, Captain. I know this isn't a choice assignment, but you pull it off and people will notice. They'll be grateful, if you understand. Sorry that everything seems to be so haphazard."

"Thank you, Colonel. I appreciate your words." He turned and trotted to the chopper, climbing the ramp into the rear of the aircraft. Once he was buckled in his seat, the crew chief raised the ramp.

Through the round windows of the fuselage, Bromhead could see a cloud of swirling dust and debris as the chopper picked up to a hover. It tilted and spun, the sunlight flashing through the portholes. Then the aircraft began to move across the airfield. The scream of the engines increased and almost drowned out the popping of the twin, heavy-duty rotor system.

They stopped moving, hanging in the air just above the ground, the dirt swirling about them, and then the nose dropped and they picked up speed to begin the climb.

2

QUI NHON, RVN

They had been airborne for more than three hours when the pitch in the Chinook's engines changed and Bromhead realized that they were descending. He opened his eyes to see the sun touching the horizon, bathing everything in bright oranges and fiery reds.

The crew chief sat next to him and yelled over the noise, "We're going to land for refueling. It'll be a couple of hours before we take off again if we want to hit the LZ at dawn."

"Where are we?" asked Bromhead.

"Qui Nhon."

"Qui Nhon? That's on the coast."

"Yes, sir. Given the time frame, it made sense for us to stop here. Besides, they've got one hell of an enlisted personnel club. Serves steaks an inch thick, beer in buckets and all the French fries you can eat. Not to mention the waitresses who wear very little because it's warm inside."

"Great," said Bromhead.

The crew chief got up and made his way to the forward section of the aircraft. Bromhead glanced across the fuselage. Gilman had stretched out, his hat over his eyes. Hansen was kneeling near the equipment, checking to see what they had.

A moment later the aircraft bounced and the crew chief reappeared as the engine whine died. "AC said that we had four hours here. Grab some food or whatever, but be back here by midnight."

Gilman pulled his hat off his eyes. "You have any plans, Captain?"

"No. Didn't know we were going to land."

"Well then, sir, come with me. I'll take you to that club where the steaks are thick, the beer is ice cold, and the women nearly naked."

The last thing Bromhead wanted to do was sit in a hot, smoky club with a bunch of drunken soldiers and sailors, but he didn't want to alienate his new men. There had been no time to get to know them. He had been thrown together with them and told that he would be working with them behind enemy lines. They would have to support one another and each would depend on the other. It was not a situation that Bromhead liked. Now that Gilman had made the first move he would have to respond and he didn't want to give the impression that he thought he was better than either Gilman or Hansen.

"Okay," said Bromhead. "But I'll buy the beer."

The big Marine clapped his hands together and nearly shouted, "You got a deal there, sir. Hey, Hansen, you going to join this party or you going to be a fucking stick-in-the-mud like last night?"

Hansen shrugged his shoulders but didn't look at Gilman. "There's work to be done right here. I think I'll just stick around."

"Hell, man," said Gilman. "You got to eat."

"We've got cases of C-rations."

"Jesus Christ!" said Gilman, laughing. "Fucking C-rats when you can have steak, probably the last you'll see in a long time. Well, don't say we didn't ask."

"Okay, Hansen," said Bromhead. "We'll leave our weapons here and you watch them. We won't travel too far from the club so that if anything comes up, you'll be able to find us."

Hansen grinned. "Yes, sir."

Bromhead was on his feet and moving toward the hatch. He stopped and turned. "Listen, I've had it with this 'yes sir' crap. Can we, for my sake, suspend it for a while, at least until we get into the field?"

"Certainly," said Gilman.

"Then let's get this show on the road."

In the fading sun, the lights of the base were barely discernible. Some of them were single bulbs that glowed dimly, others were bright, marking the edges of the airfield or one of the many clubs. Bromhead wondered about it but realized that Charlie didn't have any air power so that blackout regulations didn't mean much. Later, after midnight, the number and brightness of the lights were probably reduced to inhibit the enemy mortar crews who needed aiming stakes more than they needed lights.

They crossed the airstrip, a runway of PSP surrounded by dirt taxiways, and walked out onto a dirt road. To the right was a low building that seemed to pulse with the throbbing beat of rock music. Outside the building a group of men sat drinking beer from cans, smoking and talking noisily among themselves.

Gilman pushed past them and dragged Bromhead into the building as the music died and the swell of conversation rose. The interior was everything that Bromhead had expected. Small tables crowded together, a bar that dominated one side of the room with men four deep around it, and a jukebox on a raised platform where two soldiers stood reading the selections and feeding quarters into it.

The atmosphere in the room was hot and thick with cigarette smoke that immediately burned the eyes. Overhead,

three ceiling fans rotated but did nothing to circulate the air
or dissipate the smoke. There were nearly two dozen waitresses pushing their way among the men, some of them carrying trays with drinks, while others balanced platters of food
deftly above the crowd. Each was dressed in a tiny skirt that
displayed ruffled panties as she moved and tight-fitting blouses
cut low to reveal flashes of breast.

Gilman grinned as one of the waitresses pushed by him. He
swung a big hand at her backside, missing it by inches.

A voice from the left stopped them. "You've got to be an E-
5 or above to use this facility, gentlemen." The speaker was a
fat, balding man with a cigar clamped between his teeth.

Gilman took the wallet from his pocket and flashed his ID
card. "This do it?"

"For you, yes. What about him?"

"He's my guest."

"Yeah. Okay."

Gilman shouldered his way in, found a table just as two men
vacated it. He grabbed a waitress by the arm and yelled over
the growing din, fueled by the tunes beginning on the jukebox, "Bring us a couple of beers."

Bromhead dropped into the chair opposite him, leaned forward on the table, but didn't speak. He watched the ebb and
flow of the crowd, listening to the blaring music, raucous
laughter and swearing soldiers.

"You shouldn't have that wallet," said Bromhead, "especially with your ID card in it."

"Military regulations require that we carry the Form Two,
military ID card, wear our ID tags, and do not carry con-
cealed weapons."

"Not on a covert mission. Before we get into the field, you're
going to have to destroy that."

Gilman studied him for a moment. "Yes, sir."

"Okay, why don't you wait here while I go see if I can scare up a medic? That asshole Petersen promised one at Bien Hoa and didn't deliver."

Gilman, happy that the subject was changed from his ID card, said, "You sure we need a medic?"

"If you get wounded, who do you want treating you? Me, or a fully qualified medic?"

"I see your point." He was silent until the music died again. "You want to eat here?"

"Why not? Couple of steaks or whatever."

The drinks arrived. As Gilman leaned close to the waitress, he could see that she was sweating heavily, her clothes almost drenched.

Bromhead drained his glass in a long gulp and then stood. "I'll be back in a little while. Give me about thirty minutes and then order the dinner. Steak, rare. Potato baked, with butter, and a beer."

"Yes, sir."

Bromhead returned a few minutes before the waitress brought the food. He explained to Gilman that he'd had no luck, but one major promised to try to help. He hoped to have someone out to the airfield by midnight.

Gilman thanked the waitress, who flashed a practiced smile, then disappeared. "So," he asked Bromhead, "this your first tour in Vietnam?"

Bromhead knew what Gilman was asking. Not if it was his first tour, but if he had any experience. Gilman wanted to make sure that he wasn't going into combat with a man who hadn't been there before.

Bromhead grinned. "I have good news and bad news. I've only been here for a couple of months." He saw the expression on Gilman's face change and added quickly, "But I've been here once before for a year and a half."

"Then you know the score, sir."

Now Bromhead didn't know whether he should be insulted or not. It wasn't the place of the NCOs to question the assignment of the officers. Then he remembered something he had been told by an enlisted man a couple of years earlier. It was his life on the line, too, and sometimes he had ideas that made sense. It was only a complete idiot who didn't listen to the enlisted men just because they held a lower rank.

"I've been around for a while, if that's what you mean."

"Yes, sir. Anyway, this is my second tour and I want to make sure that I have the opportunity for a third."

"You want a third tour?" asked Bromhead.

"No, just the opportunity for one. There is a difference. After the first tour, I didn't expect to be back. For a while there, I didn't expect to leave."

"What happened?"

"Got trapped on a hilltop with about twenty other Marines while it seemed that the entire army of North Vietnam tried to overrun us. Spent the night beating back the enemy and treating each other for wounds. Artillery was raining down around us as our boys tried to stop the assaults, and enemy mortars kept dropping on us in answer to the cannon cockers." Gilman took a deep drink of his beer.

Bromhead didn't know what to say. Some men considered it impolite to ask questions about past actions. Some men repressed them, preferring to pretend that it never happened. Others wanted to talk about it, share it with men who understood the feelings. Understood how it was possible to shoot someone at close range and not feel guilt.

Gilman was opening up and it was something that Bromhead didn't want to stop. There were questions he could ask but he wasn't sure that Gilman wanted them asked.

And then the spell was broken. They began to eat, but didn't talk. The jukebox, fed with a continual stream of coins from the parade of men, drowned out conversation. Around eight, the bartender unplugged the jukebox and turned on the club's stereo system with its concert hall speakers. As the driving beat shook the building one of the waitresses, newly attired in a long dress, gloves and high-heel shoes, began dancing. Slowly she removed her clothes until she wore only the shoes, a G-string, and a garter belt with fishnet stockings. Her fingers dipped into her G-string, pulling out cotton balls that she tossed at the roaring crowd.

When they finished eating, Gilman went to the bar and got two more beers. On his return, he stopped next to a waitress in an incredibly short skirt and whispered something to her. She smiled and nodded enthusiastically.

Gilman suggested that they drink the beer outside, and they left the club. Bromhead found a spot under a tree and sat on the bench, letting the cool breeze from the ocean wash over him. There was a hint of salt in the air and the odor of fish, but after the steam-bath heat of the club and the stench of cigarette smoke, it was a welcome relief. He felt the sweat drying quickly.

Bromhead noticed that Gilman had rolled up the sleeves of his fatigues, revealing a tattoo on his forearm, the birdy on the ball, the insignia of the Marine Corps. That told Bromhead something about the man. But it was also one more way for the group to be identified as Americans, if the enemy got a chance to examine the bodies. Bromhead decided that he didn't think much of Colonel Petersen and the people who had planned the mission. Obviously they had consulted no one from the Special Forces.

The other unknown was Hansen. He didn't seem to be the type to end up in a mountain village teaching the Meos how to fight the VC and NVA. A conscientious man, but not a soldier at heart, because a real soldier wouldn't have joined the Air Force. A man interested in aviation would, but not someone who thought like a ground-pounder. Bromhead figured it would be up to him and Gilman to do the fighting. Bromhead wanted to ask more about the battle that Gilman had mentioned, but as they drank, the opening never came.

Neither said much. Both seemed to be enjoying the music playing softly in the distance. When they finished, they left the bottles on the ground but stayed where they were. Neither seemed anxious to return to the airfield.

A little later, the waitress that Gilman had spoken to slipped out the door. She hesitated there, brushing the sweat-damp hair from her forehead and ignoring the shouts and whistles from the men near her. She looked around, spotted Gilman and raised a hand in acknowledgment as she came toward him.

Gilman hopped up and held out a hand. When she was near, he said, "This is Lim. I have a date with her."

Bromhead stood and bowed slightly. "Very nice to meet you, Lim."

She smiled and cast her eyes down shyly. "Thank you," she said in heavily accented English.

Bromhead dropped back onto the bench and Gilman waited until Lim had perched herself on the edge of a wooden crate that someone had dragged over as a makeshift chair.

"Well, Lim," said Gilman sitting across from her, "how long have you worked here?"

"I been here three month," she said, grinning. Her teeth were nearly perfect, the only defect being a gap between the two front teeth. As she leaned forward, her elbows on her knees, her skirt rode higher, revealing the flawless skin of her thighs.

"Working in the club all that time?" asked Gilman.

"I dance there. Yes." She crossed her legs very slowly, watching the eyes of both men. Then she sat up straight, pulling her shoulders back so that the material of her blouse stretched across her small breasts. It was obvious that she wore no bra. Her nipples strained against the fabric.

"Dance and waitress," said Gilman.

"That right. I do both. Before I hootch maid. Clean room and shine boot."

"Are you from this area? Qui Nhon?" asked Bromhead.

"I from Tuy Phouc. My father and mother there. They farm but I do not like that. Too hard. I come here and get good job. I make much money."

Gilman stood suddenly and seized her hand. She smiled up at him but didn't stand. "I think we'll take a walk," said Gilman.

"I'll be right here," said Bromhead.

Now Lim stood and followed Gilman to a large bush, partially in the shadows. They disappeared behind it and then, a moment later, Lim stood where Bromhead could see her. She was looking down, as if studying something on the ground, as she slowly unbuttoned her blouse, shrugging it from her shoulders. It fell away, and then she unzipped her tiny skirt. She slipped it over her hips. Now there was only a wisp of paleness around her and she pushed that down her thighs to her knees. She ran a hand through her long, thick hair so that it all hung down her back to her waist. Then she turned so that she was facing Bromhead, letting him examine her nearly naked body.

Even in the half-light outside the club, he could tell that she had a fine body. Small breasts that were beautifully sculptured with large, dark nipples. An hourglass shape and then a tangle of dark hair. She grinned at him and then vanished again, crouching behind the bush.

There was a cooing, then a giggle and a sigh of pure pleasure. For a moment there was quiet and then a quiet, rhythmic slapping of flesh on flesh that began slowly but increased in tempo. There was another sigh and then a moan that was drawn out into a cry of pleasure. It grew steadily, peaked and dropped off into silence.

A moment later Lim reappeared wearing her skirt and her unbuttoned blouse. She was carrying her panties in her hand. She dropped to the bench next to Bromhead and twisted around so that he could see her breasts, her knee touching his hip.

"You like?"

"More than you'll know, Lim."

She spread her legs slightly, one foot on the ground and the other tucked under her. "What you mean?"

"It means I've got to get back to work. I have much to do tonight."

She looked as if she was going to cry. "You don't like Lim."

"I think you're a very nice girl, but I've got to go to work."

She pouted for a moment, then spread her blouse wide, as if cooling her chest, and then closed it slowly, buttoning it carefully. "You go to work and not know what you miss. I am very good. Best you ever find."

She stood in front of him, drew her skirt up to her waist and then slowly stepped into her panties. She wiggled from side to side, watching Bromhead all the while, as the underwear finally covered her genital area. She yanked them tight, snapped the waistband, then smoothed her skirt over her hips. Without a word, she spun and trotted back to the club.

As she left, Gilman stepped close. "She's very good."

Bromhead already knew that. It had taken quite an effort to ignore the show she put on for him. To Gilman he said, "I think it's time we returned to the aircraft."

"If you insist, sir."

When they got to the airfield, the flight crew was still missing, and there was no sign of a medic. Hansen was sitting in the cargo compartment, reading a paperback by flashlight. He looked up, acknowledged their presence with a nod, then turned his attention back to the book.

"Anybody been by here?" asked Bromhead.

"No, sir," replied Hansen. "It's been very quiet. Jeep drove by once but when I looked out the hatch, he took off without a word."

"Damn." Bromhead thought about calling the major again and asking the status of the search for a medic, but knew it would do no good. The man would either find him a medic in time or he wouldn't, and calling wouldn't help him.

Bromhead lay down on the troop seat, and put an arm over his eyes. He tried to tune out the noise around him, including the roar of aircraft engines, the pop of rotor blades and even the chattering of machine guns on the bunker line. The heat no longer bothered him that much although he unbuttoned his fatigue shirt, letting it hang open.

The flight crew came aboard just before midnight and went about their duties. The crew chief woke Bromhead, instructed him to strap in. They would be taking off soon. Bromhead inquired if the medic had arrived, but the crew chief knew nothing about any medic. They were almost ready to take off with one more stop scheduled at a small Special Forces camp at Dak Sut. This was necessary so that they would not be too early to the landing zone in Laos.

Once they were airborne, Bromhead went back to sleep. He was awakened just before landing and watched the approach to the darkened hillside. There was jungle all around and in the center of a gray patch a single flashing light.

When the aircraft touched down, Bromhead moved to the rear and checked through the equipment. He pulled out his rucksack and pistol belt. There were three canteens hung on it, all of them empty. As the roar from the engines died, Bromhead approached the crew chief. "How long will we be here?"

"Awhile. Why?"

"Need to get my canteens filled and my pack ready. And talk to the Detachment CO."

"Shouldn't be a problem. The sneaky Petes inside will help with the water and tell you where the CO is."

Within twenty minutes Bromhead was back and in a black mood. Like almost every Special Forces camp in South Vietnam, this one had been stripped of personnel by MACV-SOG to make up the various details for Project Delta. One of the first men taken had been the senior medic from the camp. That left them with one and the CO wasn't going to give him up. Bromhead thanked him and cursed Petersen. The fucking, ground-pounding leg didn't understand that a medic was essential.

Back at the aircraft, Bromhead sorted through his equipment, made up his pack, keeping it light since they would be relocating to the village quickly. Then he sat in the darkened interior of the aircraft to wait. He tried not to think about Petersen, except as he might look dangling at the end of a rope after the skin had been slowly peeled from his body.

Hansen, who had gone to the Special Forces commo bunker to make a radio check, returned a few minutes later. He played his flashlight around the interior of the aircraft and then switched it off.

"You ready for this mission, Captain?" he asked, trying to strike up a conversation.

Bromhead looked toward the sound, but could only see a dark lump where Hansen sat. "As ready as I'll ever be."

"Yeah, I know what you mean."

Hansen didn't say any more and after a while, Bromhead heard a snore. He grinned and then lay down. Gilman returned a short while later, but didn't speak. They all were silent then, each lost in his own thoughts. Bromhead wanted to say something, give them a last minute pep talk, but didn't know what to say to them. He didn't know the men with him and that worried him, just as it had worried Gilman.

When the flight crew returned from the mess hall, they went through the preflight procedure again. This time, when they were airborne, Bromhead didn't lie down. He watched the landscape under the aircraft but could see little in the darkness. A ribbon of silver that marked a river, or a thread of black that was a road. There were splatterings of dark gray that signified villages, some of them with scattered lights, and patterns of flat black that marked thick jungle around them. Bromhead watched them all, searching for the flashes of enemy weapons and the lines of tracers climbing toward them. He saw nothing.

Suddenly Bromhead saw a blinking red light outside the aircraft. He moved forward and tapped the crew chief on the shoulder. "What's that?"

"Escort aircraft. To make sure that we hit the right place. The AC is in touch with an AWACS aircraft that is using various electronic devices to pinpoint the LZ. The aircraft you see out there is going to lead us in."

"Great," said Bromhead. "Just what we need on a covert mission." He moved back to his seat to wait.

Within minutes the crew chief was standing near him and yelling over the sound of the engines. "We're about five out. Get ready."

Bromhead joined Gilman and Hansen at the rear of the aircraft. Two crewmen also came up to them. Bromhead was about to ask how much longer when he felt his stomach reach his throat as they began a rapid descent. It seemed that they were plunging to the ground. Bromhead's hand shot out in reflex, grabbing one of the support legs of the troop seats.

There was a sudden increase in gravity and Bromhead felt himself forced down. An instant later the pressure let up as the aircraft bounced once then settled to the ground. The crew chief ran back as one of the other crewmen hit the switch to lower the ramp.

"Go. Go. Go!" yelled the crew chief as he flipped open the buckles on the cargo belts that held the pallets in place.

Bromhead grabbed his weapon and his duffel bag and leaped out of the open hatch. He landed on the soft ground, scrambled to the edge of the jungle and halted. Over his shoulder, he could see that Gilman had taken a position on the other side of the LZ while Hansen helped to discharge the equipment. Quickly, they had it piled at the bottom of the ramp and the crewmen had disappeared inside. The engine noise increased and the aircraft rose, the rotor wash swirling around the LZ, kicking up anything that was loose. The sound faded as the helicopter climbed out, the engines belching streaks of fire.

Then the chopper was gone and the quiet became eerie. The silence was so deep that Bromhead wondered if something had gone wrong with his hearing until he heard a piercing scream, probably from some animal awakened by the helicopter.

Bromhead settled down to wait. He glanced to the east and saw the first faint fingers of dawn reaching into the sky. Overhead, in the jungle canopy, scrambling noises drew Bromhead's attention. He hoped that it was a monkey disturbed by the chopper. He looked up, but could see nothing in the darkness.

Unsnapping the camouflage cover on his watch, he lifted it to check the time and then refastened it. He turned toward the LZ, but could only make out a pale lump at one end where the equipment had been pushed. He let his eyes shift over the jungle, listened to the light rustling of leaves as a breeze blew through, but there was no evidence of humans.

Suddenly he realized that he could pick out individual trees and bushes and that the jungle had become gray instead of black. There were patches of mist drifting among the trees, making it look as if the jungle was on fire. The sky was now light gray. Bromhead got to his feet and drifted back into the LZ.

"Okay, we've got a lot of work to do today." Bromhead spoke quietly, his voice barely above a whisper, but the two NCOs heard him.

When they were grouped around the equipment, Bromhead unfolded his map, now that it was bright enough to read. He was about to speak when the jungle exploded into a riot of sound. Monkeys were howling at each other, birds were screeching and parrots squawking. Each of the men dived for cover, their weapons at the ready, but there was nothing to shoot at. They could see the animals running through the treetops, shaking the branches, screaming.

For twenty minutes the noise kept up, louder than the inside of the helicopter. They could hear nothing unless they were right next to one another, shouting directly into each other's ear. But they couldn't hold a three-way conversation.

Then, as abruptly as it started, the noise ended. Through the early morning mists, Bromhead could see no movement. Everything settled down, as if the creatures had gone into hiding.

Bromhead got his men together again, the map spread out on the top of a crate. "We're supposed to be here and the village is supposed to be here. Two klicks at the most. I'll head off to make contact with the villagers. You two stay here and guard the equipment. I suggest you do it from the jungle. Watch it, but don't sit on it. I expect to be back before noon with enough men to move everything into the ville."

Gilman spun the map so that he could look at it. He traced a route to the ville and then the line of a river. "If you don't return by noon?"

"Then you take charge. You can do one of two things. Either try to make contact with the villagers or E and E to South Vietnam."

"What do you suggest, sir?" asked Gilman.

"That you try to find me before you bug out, but as I say, that's up to you."

"Yes, sir."

Bromhead slapped Gilman on the shoulder. "Now you got it." He looked at his watch, the camouflage now folded back. "I make it ten of five."

"So you have seven hours to the ville and to get back here," said Hansen.

"Right."

Bromhead folded the map and stuffed it into a side pocket. He shouldered his rucksack and buckled his pistol belt. He then checked the magazine on his weapon, an old M-1 carbine and chambered a round. As he set the safety, he said, "Seven hours and then you're on your own."

"Yes, sir," said Gilman. "Good luck."

With that, Bromhead crossed the LZ and entered the trees to the north. He halted just inside the tree line and crouched near a giant bush with huge leaves and large pink flowers. He glanced to the right where a thorn-covered vine climbed the trunk of a tree, strangling the life from it. Overhead, the canopy closed, the broad leaves of the trees intertwining to form an unbroken roof. To the rear, he could see a patch of blue and the shafts of light from the sun. Water dripped down from the top, running along the broad leaves of the plants and down the trunks of the trees. It splashed on Bromhead, soaking his already sweat-damp uniform. As he wiped his sleeve across his forehead, he could smell the moist dirt. The dank odor reminded him of summer and his mother's fruit cellar. He knew the day was going to be hot and muggy, with the humidity draining everyone's strength.

Rising to his feet, Bromhead found a narrow game trail and began to follow it. He knew that inside Laos the VC and NVA would not booby trap the trails or lay ambushes because the Americans and South Vietnamese were not supposed to be there. Booby traps would be more of a hindrance to the Communists than to the Americans.

Bromhead crouched so that he could move along the tunnel created by the tightly intertwined bushes. The ground was soft and damp, his footprints filling with water as he made his way along the trail. He reached out to push a vine aside and immediately felt a burning sensation. He jerked his hand back and saw a red welt forming on the skin of his hand. With the barrel of his carbine, he pushed the vine out of the way and ducked under, careful not to let it touch him. From that point, he used the rifle to brush aside any vegetation that blocked his way.

Within minutes he was tired, hot and thirsty. His pace slowed as he began to climb. His mouth hung open as if he couldn't get enough air and his lungs ached. It was almost as if he had run a klick or two instead of only a hundred meters. His condition was due in part to being in the jungle again, and part of it was due to the altitude. He was three or four thousand feet above sea level where the air was thinner. Before leaving on the mission, he should have demanded a couple of weeks for conditioning.

He worked his way deeper into the twilight of the jungle. There were occasional patches of sunlight where there were tiny breaks in the thick canopy, but those were few. The deeper he went, the dimmer it became, until he was in a world of perpetual twilight.

After thirty minutes he stopped and took out his map, but the jungle was so dense there were no landmarks visible. Just mahogany, teak, palm and coconut trees. Some of these grew nearly two hundred feet tall, others shorter. Then there were bushes and brush that clung to the ground. And a small stream that wasn't marked on the map.

Bromhead pulled out his compass, sighted on a distinctive tree, a dead teak that was turning gray, and headed toward it.

When he got there, he stopped long enough to drink from his canteen, and waste a little water on his go-to-hell rag. He made another sighting, then started off again. Two hours later, he decided that he had missed the village. Suddenly he heard voices to his right. He dropped to the ground, listening and realized that they weren't speaking Vietnamese. He crawled forward slowly, easing his way among the bushes and trees, being careful not to make noise.

The jungle thinned abruptly, the broad-leafed plants and lacy ferns giving way to thick grass two or three feet tall. Bromhead found a rotting log and used it for cover. Craning, he could see into the village. Thatched hootches sat on stilts with notched logs leading to them. Some were surrounded by fences of woven branches and fires burned near others. Bare-chested women with bright clothes wrapped around their waists, tended the fires. Men wearing loose loincloths walked around chasing pigs, chickens and children. He could see stagnant pools of water and the odor of an uncovered sewer assaulted his nostrils.

Bromhead watched the village for a moment, wondering if this could possibly be the right place. The report had suggested that the French had taught them about slit trenches, penning the animals, and personal hygiene. The report had outlined how the French had brought civilization to the area. Either the villagers had forgotten the training, or this was the wrong place.

And there was no evidence of military discipline. The report had said that the ville had been organized into a strike force, but none of the men wore anything that looked like a uniform. There was no evidence of weapons, other than a machete carried by one man and a crossbow held by another.

Bromhead wasn't sure what to do. He took out his map and checked it carefully. According to it, there were no other villages close, but that didn't mean much. A thatch hootch didn't take long to construct and the fluid nature of the war could easily force the villagers to relocate. There was no guarantee that this was the right place, or if it was the right place, that it was the right group of people. The natives sometimes built their villages on the sites of old, deserted hamlets.

Bromhead decided he had no choice. Even if this was the wrong place, he would have to make contact. Slowly he got to his feet until he was standing in full view. When no one seemed to notice him, he began to walk forward. As he moved he slipped his weapon to his shoulder using the sling. He kept his hands held high where they were easily visible to anyone who wanted to look.

He was within ten yards of the village when someone spotted him. There was a shout of alarm and three of the men ran forward, forming a human wall in front of the village. Bromhead halted, grinned and shouted in French, "Greetings. I bring you assistance and weapons."

3

MEO VILLAGE
SOUTHEASTERN LAOS

For a moment they all stood there looking at one another. The women gathered the children and fled toward the rear of the village until they were out of sight. A dog, hidden under one of the hootches, began to bark. No one spoke, although one of the males was swinging his machete in tiny circles.

Bromhead spoke again in French. "Greetings," he said, and was tempted to add, "from the people of the United States," but that was supposed to be something of a secret. He tried to think of something else to say, but his limited French, taken in high school and his first year of college, and only augmented in a limited fashion by the Army, deserted him.

The men began jabbering among themselves. Another three males joined them. One of the original group came forward. A short, skinny man with long, thick greasy hair. He was covered with mud, had extremely long fingernails, and blue eyes. There was a ragged, puckered scar on his shoulder so that his left arm hung at an almost impossible angle. He held a hand up and began speaking to Bromhead slowly and distinctly in a language that Bromhead couldn't understand.

Bromhead had only been in the village for a few minutes and it already seemed to be a disaster. He couldn't communicate with anyone and the natives didn't look all that friendly. One of them kept eyeing his M-1, as if he expected to take it off Bromhead's body. Another kept his machete in motion, drawing Bromhead's attention to the blade. It looked incredibly sharp.

Bromhead tried it again. He held up a hand, palm out in a friendly manner, and said, "Greetings. I have arrived to help in the war against the Vietcong and North Vietnamese. I have weapons and equipment."

There was some response from the men. They looked at one another and spoke among themselves rapidly in a singsong language. Bromhead didn't like the way the situation was developing. He let his right hand drop to his side where he unsnapped the strap on his holster, which held a Browning M-35 9 mm pistol, his eyes locked on those of the man standing in the middle.

Then suddenly, from somewhere in the village, a feminine voice shouted in English, "Who in the hell are you?"

Everyone turned. A woman, dressed like the natives, bare to the waist with a brightly colored cloth knotted around her waist appeared. She had blond hair that hung in a tangle. There were tan lines on her breasts and she wore sandals. She was taller than the natives by a good four inches. She stopped walking, ran a hand through her hair, pushing it away from her face, and then put a hand on her hip.

"I asked, who in the hell are you?"

Bromhead was momentarily stunned. He hadn't been ready for a white woman to appear among the natives; one who spoke English and who seemed to have her own ideas. The rest of the women remained hidden, this one was now standing behind the men, a hand on her hip. Remembering his directive that demanded silence, Bromhead merely said, "I'm Bromhead. Jack Bromhead."

"And what in the hell are you doing here?"

"I've been sent to provide, ah, aid for these people." He found himself staring at her breasts. They were a golden brown while her shoulders and stomach were quite dark. They were firm, well-shaped breasts and as he watched, the nipples grew erect. He tried to pull his eyes away but couldn't.

She noticed his gaze and was suddenly embarrassed by it. She raised her hands, dropped them and then tried to casually fold her arms over her chest, hiding herself.

"Who are you?" he asked.

"I'm Jane Lucas." She recrossed her arms, splaying her fingers out to hide her nipples. "I'm studying the culture and internal structure of the Meo. I've a grant from the National Endowment for the Sciences. I've been here for twelve weeks. Arrived with the help of the Laotian government, on that grant. A legal grant. Here to study these people in their natural habitat."

Bromhead realized that she was babbling. Maybe she was embarrassed by being caught seminude. He let his eyes fall to the ground and found himself staring at her ankles. Very trim ankles that were smeared with dirt.

The man with the scarred shoulder began speaking, first to Lucas in Meo, his voice rising and falling harshly, and then to one of the men. He was taller and stockier than the rest and wore only black shorts. His hair was braided. He said something in a sharp, quiet voice. The woman looked at him, stood her ground for a moment and then spun, stomping off. Bromhead watched her retreat.

In French, the man said, "You have brought weapons?"

"Yes. Many. And other equipment. Things that you need and you can have, all of it stored close to the village. We have a great deal of work to do.'' He kept his eyes on Lucas until she disappeared around a corner.

''Then let us get started,'' said the man. He faced the village and put his hands to the sides of his mouth, yelling in a high-pitched, warbling voice. He kept the call going, sounding as if he was calling the men to a prayer meeting.

People began to appear from inside the hootches, out of the jungle, and from behind the fences and near the scattered trees. They formed a ragged line behind the tall man, looking as if they were trying to remember their military lessons. A couple of them stood with their crossbows at their sides. One man held a rifle with a stock made from bamboo.

Bromhead moved down the line like a general reviewing his troops. He glanced at each man and the weapon he held, trying to ignore the odor of unwashed humanity that radiated from the villagers. Each of them was smeared with dirt, their feet black. One of the first things that Bromhead would have to do was institute a program of cleanliness.

When he finished, he walked back to the headman and stopped. He was anxious to suggest that they set up a guard system, get a roving patrol into the jungle to watch for the enemy, and to start a regular program of patroling so that they wouldn't be surprised. He wanted to get things cleaned up and start on building bunkers. There were a hundred things that needed to be done immediately but it wasn't the time. He would have to learn patience. He couldn't get it all done in one day. There would have to be a program of priorities so that he didn't drive himself crazy trying to do too much too soon.

''I will need,'' he told the man who seemed to be the leader, ''thirty men to help move the equipment from the landing zone to your village. We will need a place to store it, and then I will want to talk to all the men who have received some kind of military training.''

The leader nodded through the speech and then spun, trying to execute an about-face. With his hands at his sides, he shouted at the men in their language. He pointed at them, splitting them into two groups. When he was finished, he turned back to Bromhead. ''We go now.''

''Okay,'' said Bromhead in English. He had hoped for a chance to look around the village before they went after the equipment, but that couldn't be done. Besides, there were no signs of any other military presence. The only problem was the white woman, but it was a problem he would have to deal with later. Now the headman was anxious to get moving, and so was Bromhead.

He nodded at the headman and then spoke in French. ''Form the men into a line. I will take the point. I want three men at the end of the line as a rear guard. You understand?''

''I have it.'' He grinned, displaying broken and yellowed teeth.

Bromhead unslung his carbine, thought about it, and then handed it to the headman. ''You carry this,'' he said. ''I'll use my pistol.''

Bromhead led them to the game trail that he had used to find the camp. He promised himself that it was something he would never do again in South Vietnam. In the combat environment of Vietnam, using the same trail twice was the quickest way to get ambushed and eliminated. But this wasn't South Vietnam and not a combat environment. The enemy didn't expect the Americans to be operating in Laos and weren't looking for them. Once they had their camp established and began military operations, Bromhead would have to be careful about violating the rules, but at this moment, the quickest route was the best.

Once they were into the jungle, away from the village, Bromhead stopped long enough to review the column. It was obvious that the men had had some military training, and as they fanned out through the trees, that training was coming back. They didn't bunch up, and although they were talking, they kept their voices down. Not absolute noise discipline, but like the rest, Bromhead ignored it for the moment.

They filtered through the jungle, moving down to the LZ. It was an easier trip for Bromhead. He kept the pace rapid and didn't give them a break. When he was close to the LZ, he halted them and entered it on his own. Once Gilman and Hansen were warned that Bromhead and his party was there, Bromhead ordered them into the LZ.

Gilman and Hansen moved to the equipment and began to separate it into loads for the men. Some of the men, using saplings cut to form poles, were able to pair up and carry a couple of crates. In just a few minutes they were ready to start the trip back to the camp. Bromhead told the headman to lead them, keep the pace steady, but make sure that they didn't get too far ahead. He wanted the column to remain together as much as possible.

As the men moved out, Bromhead grabbed Gilman. "I want you to stick here for a while. Make sure we've left nothing on the LZ that will identify us to the enemy. Then follow at a short distance so that we can get a reading on how much noise these guys make."

"I'd bet, sir, that they can glide through the jungle without a sound if they want."

"You're probably right. See if they leave any signs. Pick up anything they might drop."

"Yes, sir."

Bromhead was about to caution him about calling him sir, but then decided against it. In South Vietnam, the officers always tried to do nothing that would call attention to them. They didn't point, tried to stay clear of the radio, and didn't require saluting. But here these things might become important. It might become a way of establishing and maintaining authority. Dealing with people of different ethnic backgrounds could become a real pain in the ass.

So, instead of any of that, Bromhead said, "Just don't get yourself lost or captured here."

"Don't worry about that."

"See you at the village." Bromhead hurried after the men, joined the rear of the formation and watched them climb the trail leading home. The pace uphill seemed faster than it had been down. Bromhead wondered if the men were hurrying so that they could break into the crates and grab the weapons and ammo.

Bromhead watched the column, fascinated. The heat, humidity and altitude didn't seem to bother them. They didn't sweat, nor was any of them breathing hard. They ran up the hill, carrying the loads that should have slowed them considerably. And the closer they got to the village, the faster they seemed to move.

As they approached the village, Bromhead began to see and hear signs of it. Signs that hadn't been visible or audible in the early morning hours. Smoke from a dozen or more campfires worked its way into the sky, marking the ville. Women and children were laughing and shouting. There were bleatings and bellowing from the animals. From somewhere came the discordant music favored by some of the people of Asia. The annoying sounds penetrated the jungle and Bromhead wondered why a village that was so primitive would have a radio. It had to be battery-powered since there was no other electricity available and was probably some form of government propaganda. A gift to the poor.

They came out of the jungle, crossing the open ground toward the village. As the first group of men entered it, they were met with wild cheering. The males who had been left behind had not been idle. They had been organizing a celebration. They had selected a water buffalo and staked it in the middle of the village. They were waiting for the return of the men before they began the ritual of beating it to death.

Bromhead hurried to the head of the column to speak to the leader. "We need to store the equipment somewhere so it will be protected. Somewhere out of the rain."

"We give to the men. They protect it."

"No," said Bromhead. "First we must store it and check it all. Then as we form the strike force, we will issue the equipment. But first we must check it. We have to make sure that we got all we are entitled to."

The man nodded as if he saw the wisdom of that, and ordered his men to take the rifles and ammo and supplies to a long, empty hootch in the middle of the village. This thatched structure was used as the sleeping quarters for visitors. It was situated in the center of the ville where the men could protect it and where their visitors could sleep in safety.

Bromhead moved to the interior of the hootch to watch the men bring in the boxes. He didn't want anyone raiding the equipment. Issuing it would become a ritual to mark the completion of a portion of the training. It would be a reward for a job well done. If he allowed the men to steal from him, it would undermine what he needed to do.

The interior of the hootch was bare. The floor of split logs was rough and through gaps in it, he could see the ground. The thatch was thick and there was a platform of blackened stone at one end for a fire. Part of the wall was reinforced with stone and there was a hole in the roof for the smoke to escape. Bromhead suspected that the hootches for guests burned down frequently if people built fires in them.

Once all the equipment was stacked inside, Bromhead left Hansen in charge to count and examine the equipment. He side-stepped a foul-smelling puddle of water, avoided a fence of woven branches loaded with thorns and approached the headman who was studying the water buffalo. To the left,

Bromhead could see the white woman, who now wore a brightly colored bra. He smiled to himself, finding it difficult to avoid staring at her. He noticed that she had washed herself and combed her hair. It was pulled back off her face in a ponytail.

The headman spoke in French. "When all your men arrive, we will begin the celebration."

Bromhead nodded. "Shouldn't we begin getting things into a military shape?"

"Tomorrow." The man waved his hand. "We start that tomorrow. Today we celebrate the assistance we get from our friends in far away France."

Bromhead's head jerked upright at the village chief's comment. He was grinning happily. Apparently he had assumed that the French paratroopers had returned, and since the common language was French, it was a natural mistake. Bromhead decided to do nothing to change the man's opinion.

"Tomorrow we begin to train to fight the Communists. We learn how to kill them and drive them from your homeland."

"Yes."

Leaving the headman to worry about the water buffalo, Bromhead moved off, searching for Gilman. He was standing alone, watching a group of women working around a cooking pot. On Bromhead's approach, Gilman looked up.

"Let's head over to the guest hootch for a couple of minutes. I want to know what you saw on your way in."

"Sure thing," said Gilman. "Say, I have a question. How are we supposed to treat the women around here?"

Bromhead studied the huge man and then glanced past him to the diminutive women. Gilman was nearly three times as big as any of the people in the village. "Let's treat them with respect and let them take the lead. We don't want to insult them or alienate them."

Gilman shook his head sadly. "I would do nothing to insult them, sir."

"Then we have nothing to worry about."

They reached the hootch where the equipment was stored. Hansen was sitting on the floor with rifle components scattered in front of him. When he heard the others, he said, "They're all packed in grease. Before we can use them, we're going to have to clean them thoroughly."

"Good." Bromhead found a seat on a crate stenciled Hand Grenades. "That'll inhibit the men until we get established here. Now, we need to discuss a few things."

Gilman joined Hansen on the floor and took out a canteen. He drank deeply, letting some of the water run down his chin to soak into his shirt. He wiped his mouth on the back of his hand. "Go ahead, sir."

"First thing, what did you see on your way in here?"

Gilman rubbed a hand over his lips. "The LZ was clean. Hell, there were depressions in the grass where our stuff had been, but the natives grabbed everything, including the wood of the pallets and the bent nails. Some paper, but I picked that up, so once the grass springs back, no one will know we were there."

"Good. Now I think we should establish a rank structure." He held up a hand to stop any protest. "We're going to be forming a guerrilla army here. I'm going to operate as the commander with a rank of colonel. The headman will be my counterpart and be a colonel. You two will be battalion commanders with ranks of major. For the sake of appearances, you'll have to take orders from the headman. Under each of you will be two company commanders who are captains and then platoon leaders who are lieutenants."

"That's an awfully big army, Colonel," said Gilman, grinning.

"Right now we'll start with a single platoon and rely on the headman to put his best men into it. We'll tell him what we're looking for and see how he responds. It'll also give us a clue about his thinking. From there, after we've trained them, we'll draw the officers and NCOs."

"When do we start all this?" asked Hansen.

"Tomorrow. We start slowly, interviewing the men. We'll have a bit of a communication problem, but we'll be able to work around that. Just slide into it. I think the key to this whole thing is going to be patience. Don't try to take them too far too fast."

"What kind of training?" asked Gilman.

"I think it should be in two stages. On one hand we'll want to begin the military training immediately and on the other we'll want to institute a program of civic action. Get some of the filth out of here."

Gilman got up and walked around the interior of the hootch. He touched the thatch, looked at his fingers and then rubbed them on his shirt. He looked at Bromhead. "I just don't know about this. The more I think about it, the more I feel that we haven't been given the training necessary to complete this mission. They threw us into this situation and let us have our heads. I'm a fucking combat infantryman, not a fucking teacher."

"I'm afraid," said Bromhead, "that we've all become fucking teachers. We'll just have to do the best we can. Take it slow and build a strike force and a fortified camp. Teach these guys what you know. Think about what was done to you in basic training and structure your program like that. We don't have to worry about someone looking over our shoulder with a lot of bullshit regulations. That's all there is to it."

"Yes, sir," said Gilman.

"Among ourselves we can let the military courtesies slip, but in front of the natives we'll have to follow strict military training." Bromhead smiled. "The first lesson. Lead by example. Let the men see that you know how to do it right and they'll follow."

"Yes, sir."

"Okay, for tonight, let's just relax. We'll take turns going to the party. I want one of us in this hootch at all times so that no one can get into the equipment. You've got to eat and drink out there, but use some common sense. No one gets drunk."

Both Gilman and Hansen nodded.

"Tomorrow, after we have a chance to look at the men, we'll get together and plan a strategy. Any questions?"

A female voice came from the doorway.

Bromhead turned and saw Jane Lucas standing there, one hand on the thatch as she crouched to enter.

"What can I do for you?" he asked.

"Answer one question. Who are you people?"

"Just soldiers who have been given the task of assisting these people. We have been given a job to do. Training these people so that they can defend themselves from the Pathet Lao and the North Vietnamese."

She entered the hootch and looked at the pile of equipment. "Can we talk about that?"

"Sure," said Bromhead. He waved a hand at the wooden boxes. "Have a seat." He pointed at Gilman and Hansen. "Why don't you two look around outside for a few minutes? Get a feel for the layout of the village."

Lucas sat down. She had changed again and now appeared to be on safari. She wore a bush jacket complete with loops for bullets like the one favored by the Saigon journalists, a skirt that stopped well above her knee, khaki socks that reached the knee and soft leather boots. All that was missing was a pith helmet. She sat on a crate and crossed her legs slowly.

"You have to leave," she said.

"Leave? You've got to be kidding."

"No, I'm not. You're messing up my project here. I'm studying these people. Observing them in order to learn how they live. I'm trying to understand their social structure. Now you come in and give them weapons and teach them to fight a war. If you stay, you're going to destroy their social structure."

"We're not here to destroy anything or to necessarily fight a war. We're also going to teach them something about sanitation, food preservation and self-defense. Maybe show them ways to improve these structures, give them some first-aid knowledge. There is so much they need to learn. There is so much that we can do for them."

"But if you do that, then my job is wasted."

"I'm afraid I don't understand." He remembered the way she had looked as he had entered the village, dressed like the natives and covered with dirt.

"To study these people, I have to gain their trust. To do that, I have to live with them, live like them and become one of them. It isn't right to bring them into your war. They want no part of your war and can understand nothing about it. It isn't right to pretend that your way of life is the correct one and everyone should live that way."

"Look, Jane. May I call you that?"

She nodded. "Please."

"Jane, I, too, have a job to do here. It's not as cut and dried as you may think. I'm not here to bring the war to these people, but to assist them if it should arrive."

"But don't you see? I can't do mine if you're out there changing everything. One of the rules I operate under is that I don't interfere in their life. I study and watch, but I don't participate."

Bromhead shook his head. "How can you do that? How can you sit by and let them do things that you know are going to make them sick or injure them? How can you sit back and let the sick die when you know how to treat the disease?''

"Because I don't make moral judgments," she said. "That is not my place. Who is to say that their way of life is inferior to ours?''

Bromhead looked at the floor. He breathed deeply and then glanced up. He thought Jane Lucas was an attractive, intelligent woman. He wanted to be able to tell her what she wanted to hear, but it was impossible. There was no way he could pack up and get out. He said, "I'm not making any judgments. I'm here to help these people. Give them a way to protect themselves from the VC, teach them ways to prevent sickness . . ."

"To involve these people in a war that they aren't involved in?''

"Oh? Is that a fact? I saw a few people with scars that suggest they are shrapnel and bullet wounds. I noticed that the men knew a little bit about military operations. They knew how to march through the jungle in military fashion. Somebody has been here teaching them something. I would suggest that these people have already been involved in a war. And I'll bet they'll be involved again, whether we stay or not."

"I've been here for twelve weeks and I haven't seen a sign of your feared Communists. That's just an excuse for you. A reason to get these people involved.''

Bromhead held up his hands. "What would you have me do?''

"Get out of here now while you have the chance. Leave these people alone.''

"I'm sorry. I can't do that. In fact, I might tell you to do the same thing. Get out of here. You don't belong here. There is a war going on all over this place. It has spilled from South Vietnam into Laos and Cambodia and threatens Thailand. Find someone else to study.''

Lucas stood up, her hands on her hips. "I knew I wouldn't be able to reason with you. I knew you were just another pawn of the Pentagon and don't care about anyone but yourself." She spun and headed for the door. She stopped short and added, "You're going to get a lot of these people killed. I hope you can live with yourself." With that, she disappeared.

4

MACV HEADQUARTERS, SAIGON

Captain Mack Gerber sat quietly while Master Sergeant Anthony B. Fetterman picked up the chain from the floorboards of the Army jeep and looped it through the steering wheel. Using the padlock at the end of the chain, he fastened it so that no one could turn the wheel. It was the only way they had of locking the vehicle so that it wouldn't be stolen.

When the ritual was completed, Gerber got out, grabbed his M-16 from the back, and waited. Fetterman joined him and they both headed up the wide sidewalk that led to the double doors of MACV. The MP didn't challenge them, having become used to the two of them coming and going during the last several weeks.

Once inside, the pair shivered at the sudden change in temperature as they walked down the air-conditioned and artificially lit hallway. The floor was tiled and the walls were painted a light green. They were lined with photographs of every imaginable chain of command. There were pictures of the American President and his staff, including the civilian Secretaries of Defense, the Army, Air Force and Navy. The military leaders, from the Chairman of the Joint Chiefs of Staff, through the various regional and area commanders smiled out from their official, black and white portraits.

There were also official Army posters. Some demanded that the men and women wear the uniform proudly and properly and others detailed the correct order to wear the various ribbons and decorations.

There were dozens of men and women roaming the halls. Many wore jungle fatigues that had been ironed and starched and showed no sign of sweat. Most of the women were in civilian clothes. They wore fashionably short skirts and light blouses and most of them wore sweaters because of the efficiency of the air-conditioning. Gerber thought there was something wrong here. They were living in a tropical environment where the temperature rarely, if ever, dipped to the point of coolness. The women shouldn't need sweaters to keep warm.

They reached a stairwell and descended into the basement. They were stopped by an iron gate guarded by an MP with a .45 on his hip and an M-16 within easy reach. Once again, the guard recognized them, but he demanded to see their ID cards. Satisfied, he made them sign in before he unlocked the gate. After they had been admitted, the guard locked the gate again.

They walked down a barren cinder-block hallway. The green tile floor was rust stained where metal cabinets had once stood and had since been moved. They stopped in front of a plain wooden door with nothing to indicate what was on the other side.

Without a word, Gerber knocked on the door. It was opened a moment later by a short man with dark hair and dark eyes. He had the kind of sunburned complexion that never tanned. The white suit he wore was wrinkled and stained and his thin, black tie had been loosened.

For a moment Jerry Maxwell, resident CIA man, stared balefully at them. "To what do I owe the dishonor of this visit, Gerber?"

"You see," said Gerber to Fetterman, "I told you he wouldn't be happy to see us. We help him out all the time, take missions that suck, and he's never happy to see us."

"Yes, sir. Maybe we should just trot on over to the embassy and ask our questions there. At least they are nice to us."

"That's a good idea. Maybe stop by the press office and see what they might know."

Maxwell shook his head. "It's this way every time. You guys show up with a tired comedy routine that you think is the funniest thing since the whoopy cushion."

"You going to invite us in, Jerry?" asked Gerber. "Or are you going to conduct business in the hallway where everyone in the world can listen in?"

Maxwell sighed. He stepped out of the way and waved them in. Then he closed the door. "Have a seat and tell me what you bandits want."

Gerber dropped into the chair reserved for visitors. It was a plush chair that had seen better days. Across the small office was a row of four-drawer file cabinets, the last having a large combination lock on it. Maxwell's battleship-gray desk was shoved into a corner. The side next to the wall was lined with three rows of empty Coke cans. The top of the desk was littered with manila file folders, many of them stamped top and bottom with a big, red Secret.

The only picture was an Army lithograph titled "The Wagon Box Fight" and showed the U.S. Cavalry fighting the Sioux Indians in northern Wyoming. The glass was cracked.

Fetterman moved into the corner near the file cabinets and leaned on it. He picked up a folder that lay there, saw it was classified and then opened it. "Interesting," he said.

"Put that down," said Maxwell, and then fell into his chair. He leaned his elbows on his desk and asked, "Why do I even bother?"

Gerber snatched a folder from the desk, read the label and asked, "You really interested in the standing army of Togo?"

"What's on your mind, Captain?" asked Maxwell.

"Jerry!" said Gerber, surprised. "Aren't you going to tell me that this is classified? Aren't you going to grab it out of my hand and shout at me?"

"Would it do any good?"

Gerber looked at Fetterman, who was still absorbed in the file he had found. He turned back to Maxwell. "I don't know. It might."

"I have work to do," said Maxwell.

"You always have work to do. Even when you're planning to send us into the North to steal missile guidance systems you have work to do."

Maxwell's head snapped up. "You're not supposed to talk about that."

"Even here? Don't tell me you've forgotten about it?"

"What do you want?" asked Maxwell.

Gerber turned to Fetterman. "What do we want, Master Sergeant?"

Fetterman closed the file and dropped it on the file cabinet. "What we want, Mr. Maxwell, is to find out where young Captain Bromhead has been sent and what he's doing?"

"Can't help you. I don't know where he is."

"Come on, Jerry. You know. You can tell us. We won't tell anyone that you talked," coaxed Gerber.

"You don't understand," said Maxwell. "I really don't know. Oh, I've heard some rumblings about a super-sensitive mission and knew that they had grabbed a couple of guys from various places. Bromhead mixed up in that?"

"That's what we're trying to find out," said Gerber.

Maxwell turned so that he was looking directly at Gerber. "You know, you'd be better off talking to your friends at SOG. If there is a clandestine mission going on, they'd be the ones running it."

Gerber clapped his hands together and said, "What say, Tony? Over to SOG to see who might know something?"

"I think maybe Mr. Maxwell knows something."

"Jerry?"

"If I knew anything, I'd tell you guys, just to get you the hell out of here."

Gerber got to his feet. "If you do hear anything, give me a shout, will you?"

"If I do, I will. But don't hold your breath."

"Come on, Tony, let's get out of here so that Jerry can study the military strength of Togo."

IT WAS ALMOST DUSK when the village chief announced that the meal was ready. Bromhead had watched them earlier, a dozen men with heavy clubs, as they advanced on the water buffalo. They had surrounded it and stood waiting. The animal seemed to sense something as it strained at the rope tethering it to a stake, its eyes rolling wildly as it bellowed its fright. Without a signal, the men moved in as one, striking the animal with the clubs. Smacking its flanks and back and rear. Stinging blows that rained down on the beast as it bucked and jumped, jerking its head from side to side, trying to free itself.

The men seemed to be fearless. They danced close to the animal, swung at it like a hitter going for the center field fence, and then pranced away. For thirty minutes the men kept at it. Blood stained the animal and splattered as it was hit. It fell to its knees and then to its side, the bellowing diminishing to a whimper.

The headman approached then, swung at the head and crushed the skull. As the animal died, a man with a machete ran forward, knelt in front of the beast and swung from right to left. The soft skin of the belly split, dumping the entrails into the dirt with a burst of blood and a belching of foul-smelling gases from its ruptured abdomen.

Other men, not selected to participate in the sacrifice of the animal, dug a shallow pit and started a fire. When it had burned down to glowing orange coals, they covered that with flat rocks and another layer of wood, which burned rapidly.

When the animal was dressed, its carcass was dragged to the fire pit and thrown in. The heat scorched it, burning the hair from it and sealing in the juices. A half dozen men were assigned the task of cooking the meat while the majority of the others stood around watching and drinking a home-brewed beverage, yelling at one another and laughing uproariously.

The headman found Bromhead and invited him out, giving him a gourdful of the foul-smelling liquor. Knowing that half his job was to earn the respect of the villagers, he accepted the gourd and drank deeply. It burned his throat and set his stomach on fire. For a moment he wasn't sure that he would keep it down, but the nausea passed and he grinned at the natives. They cheered, rushed forward to slap him on the back, and went on with their own drinking.

During the afternoon, Bromhead caught Lucas staring at him several times. She was on the edge of the group, standing near the corner of a hootch watching him. When he turned in her direction, she would vanish, only to reappear later near a different hootch. She didn't appear to be angry with him, or resent his intrusion. In fact, it was so bizarre, he wasn't sure what to make of it. The first time he saw her, she was wearing her safari outfit, the next time she was dressed like the native women again. He decided that the best course was to ignore her.

And then it was nearly dusk and the men were running through the village, calling to everyone, summoning them to the pit. When the crowd was gathered, the carcass was pulled from the fire and hoisted on a tall tripod. The headman, a machete in his right hand, began cutting strips of steaming meat and handing them out. The first chunk went to Bromhead, who took a huge bite, letting the juices run down his chin. The second went to Gilman and the third to a man who placed it on a palm leaf and took it to Hansen in the weapons hootch.

When the men were served, the women paraded through, taking food on palm leaves, which they used as plates, and moving off by themselves. Bromhead watched Lucas as she walked among the women. She paid no attention to him, apparently participating in the feast because the villagers were doing it and it had been their idea, and not because she approved of the new arrivals.

More food was brought out, steaming pots containing the entrails of the water buffalo, some filled with monkey and snake and a few with vegetables that grew wild. Others contained rice and more alcohol. All of it was passed around and everyone, using palm leaves for plates, helped themselves.

As the sun disappeared, fires were lit throughout the village. The men began dancing, darting among the women until nearly everyone in the village was involved in the dance. Only the headman and his three wives, Bromhead and now Hansen, and Lucas were excluded from the ceremony.

Bromhead finally got up and walked over to Lucas. He sat down next to her but kept his eyes on the dancers. In the flickering firelight, Bromhead could see the shape of her face quite well. She was bare-breasted again, but now it seemed to be a matter of defiance. She kept her attention focused on the party, refusing to acknowledge Bromhead, except with a curt nod as he sat down.

Although they didn't speak, neither of them moved. The villagers, drinking more of the obnoxious alcohol, were becoming noisier and drunker. The movements of the dance degenerated into staggering until people began collapsing into the dirt. No one paid attention to those who were passed out, dancing over them and around them. The later the hour, the more people lying on the ground.

Bromhead tried to engage Lucas in conversation several times, but she only answered with one or two word responses. The interesting thing was that she didn't move away. She sat there as if inviting conversation and then refused to participate.

Bromhead decided that he was going to wait her out. Either she was going to talk to him, or she was going to have to get up and leave. Periodically he renewed the assault, but it was always repulsed.

It was nearly midnight when Gilman appeared. "Your turn to watch the equipment, sir."

Bromhead looked at the bodies, saw a couple of men seated so that they were braced by stilts of the hootches. "I'm not sure there is anyone in the village alert enough to steal anything from us."

"Up to you, sir."

"Well, I set up the rules so I suppose I should live by them. You might want to keep an eye on the perimeter. I seriously doubt that we have anything to worry about, but let's not go to sleep, either."

Bromhead stood up and glanced at Lucas. She hadn't looked at them. She seemed fascinated by something, although the celebration had burned itself out. There was still a glow from the cooking pit, and several of the other fires were still burning brightly, throwing a flickering light over the village.

"If you'll excuse me, Jane," said Bromhead.

"Of course," she snapped, and then turned to face him. "Sorry. There is no reason to be rude."

"Yes, well." Bromhead turned and headed to the weapons hootch. As he entered, he noticed that Gilman had left a lantern burning. There was a magazine near it and Bromhead picked it up. He had hoped for something better than a worn, dog-eared copy of *Sports Illustrated*. It had to belong to Hansen because Gilman would have brought one filled with pictures of naked women.

He flipped through it and then tossed it aside. Inside one of the boxes he found a blank journal and opened it. He dated the top of the page, then began a log of the day's events, struggling to jot it down in French, and keeping it generic enough that anyone finding it wouldn't be able to use it as evidence against them. It was an accounting of the events so that Bromhead, on being debriefed, would have something to jog his memory.

He kept at it for fifteen minutes, putting everything he could think of into the journal, using it as a planning guide as well. Writing down his ideas for the training of the men. Then, as his hand was beginning to cramp, he heard a sound outside and a voice asked, "Can I come in?"

Bromhead sat up. "Yes, of course."

Jane Lucas entered, stopped and blinked at the lantern. She shook her head almost sadly. "I can't even have the luxury of a lantern. Oh, I have one for emergencies, but I don't dare use it. I have to live just as these people do."

"Seems to be an extreme way to live."

"I suppose it is." She moved into the circle of light around the lantern and sat, folding her legs Indian fashion. "I think we got off on the wrong foot."

Bromhead scratched his neck. Although it was cooler now with the sun gone, he found himself beginning to sweat. He wished he had something to do with his hands. He picked up his pencil, twisting it between his fingers. "Yes, I suppose we did."

"Some of that was my fault," Jane said. "I should have realized that you had your job just as I had mine. But now, thinking about it, I realize that we don't have to be working against one another. I realized, as we sat together watching the dancing, that we can work together."

"I'll do everything I can to cooperate," said Bromhead, "as long as it doesn't interfere with my primary function."

"Now that's what I mean," she said. "How would you like it if I came in here and told you that I would do what I could as long as it didn't interfere with my job. Besides, I was here first."

"That's not a real point, is it? You being first. I'm trying to help these people. You're here to watch. So watch."

"Mr. Bromhead, I don't think you understand. I think your presence here constitutes a danger to these people. The Communists haven't shown an interest in them in the weeks I've been here."

"All I can say," responded Bromhead, "is that I'll do what I can not to get into your way." He suddenly realized how that sounded. His job was important and hers was just something that she was doing. "Let me rephrase that. Hell, let me rethink my whole attitude here."

She smiled. "Please do."

He stood, moved from the circle of light, inspected the fire stones at the end of the hootch and then came back. He sat on the floor next to her. "Your job is to study the social structure and culture of these people. Mine is to teach them things that they're going to need to survive in the world. Does that make our jobs mutually exclusive?"

For a moment she was quiet. Then she spoke. "I'm only supposed to watch them. Observe them."

"Right. Now, if you were teaching them the things that I plan to, you'd be violating your oath or principles, or whatever, but I'm not violating mine. So you're presented with the opportunity to watch a society in the state of flux."

"You're trying very hard," she said, her attitude softening.

Bromhead reached out to touch her arm. His hand froze in midair. In the distance, outside the hootch, he heard a quiet pop. He looked at the thatched wall, hesitated and then dived across the floor, pulling Lucas to her side. As he rolled onto her, he felt her sweat-damp skin against his hand and the softness of her body. He felt her tense and then kick out with one leg.

"What the hell are you doing?" she shouted. She tried to roll to the left, away from him, and kicked. She brought her knee up sharply, but hit nothing. She levered her hands under his shoulders and tried to push him up.

"Quiet," he whispered. "Incoming."

But she wasn't quiet because she didn't understand. She struggled. She tried to get away from him, working her feet and legs and arms. Shoving and pushing and trying to bite him and force him off her.

The first explosion, a loud bang that rained debris on the village, stopped her. There was a second and a third, each louder than the last. Bromhead slipped forward, covering more of her with his body. She didn't resist.

"Coming at us," he said.

Then it seemed that the explosions had leaped over them, walking away from them. Bromhead lifted his head. "I think that's it."

He scrambled to his feet, forgetting the feeling and texture of her body. He grabbed at his weapon. "You stay here for a moment. You're safer here than you are running around in the dark."

"I told you," she admonished. "I told you you'd bring trouble down on these people."

Bromhead was out the door then. He saw Gilman coming at him. They crouched near the edge of a hootch, the light from a fire giving each of them a flickering appearance.

"You spot the flashes?" asked Bromhead.

"Think the tube is off the south. What do you want to do?"

"Leave Hansen here. We'll go out and see if we can find anything, though I doubt it. I don't like this. We're here for less than a day and we're hit the first night."

"I'll grab my belt and a couple of grenades."

Bromhead found Hansen, gave him his instructions and then joined Gilman at the edge of the village. They crouched in the darkness for a moment, watching the jungle in front of them, but saw and heard nothing. Bromhead slipped off the safety and stood, moving through the tall grass and into the jungle. He stepped around the trunk of a palm tree and it was like stepping into another world. The light from the fires seemed to go out immediately. A blackness descended hiding nearly everything. Bromhead halted, heard Gilman push a branch out of the way and saw him about two feet away. Gilman took the point, leading them both deeper into the jungle.

Bromhead stayed with him, moving with him as they worked their way toward the enemy. It wasn't easy, trying not to step on anything that would make noise. They had to keep quiet, yet they had to move quickly, before the enemy had too much time to get away.

They ducked under fallen trees held up by the thick vegetation around them. Pushing aside vines that tried to snag their uniforms, they stepped around large bushes. They veered from a trail, deeper into the jungle, listening and watching for the enemy, but the darkness blinded them. Everything was reduced to black shapes and blacker shapes. Bromhead didn't think they had a chance of finding anything, but they had to make the effort.

Bromhead was about to reach out to tap Gilman's shoulder to stop him when they heard the sound of laughter and a subdued voice telling someone to shut up in Vietnamese. Gilman halted, cocked his head to locate the sound, and turned to the right.

Without a word to Gilman, Bromhead moved farther to the right so that they were moving nearly shoulder-to-shoulder. He stopped again when he heard the quiet clank of metal against metal and a whispered order. Bromhead stepped forward, reached out to grab a branch, then froze. Immediately in front of him a shaft of moonlight cut through the jungle canopy. In a clearing there were three men crouched around a mortar tube. Bromhead couldn't believe their luck.

Before he could move, Gilman opened fire. In the strobing flashes beside him, Bromhead could see the leaves of a bush and the trunk of a tree. One of the trio dived for cover. Another screamed, a high-pitched sound.

There was a ripping sound as one of the enemy opened fire with his AK-47. The green tracers bounced through the darkness and the muzzle-flashes revealed the man.

Bromhead aimed and fired once, then dropped to the ground. He fired a second time. The enemy soldier spun and returned a burst at Bromhead, the rounds slamming into the jungle near him. Bromhead felt one of the slugs impact the tree, showering him with bark and splinters of teak.

Gilman squeezed off a couple of shots and then ran. Bromhead could hear him thrashing through the jungle as he tried to flank the enemy soldiers. Green tracers followed him as the VC fired at his fleeing form.

Bromhead crawled forward and craned his neck. One of the enemy was kneeling near the mortar tube. Bromhead looked over the sights of his weapon and pulled the trigger rapidly.

He saw the rounds connect, slamming the man backward. As he fell, the VC jerked the trigger, unleashing a burst into the sky.

The firing stopped as suddenly as it began. Bromhead let his eyes sweep over the field, but there was no movement. The only sound was a quiet moan coming from the wounded man. Bromhead didn't move. He was suddenly aware of everything around him. A stench rose from the jungle floor. Rotting vegetation mixed with damp earth. He could feel the moisture soaking through his uniform, chilling him in the cool, mountain air.

When nothing happened after a few more minutes, Bromhead slowly got to his feet. He stepped away from the trees and into the clearing. As he entered it, he crouched in order to see better. There was tall grass around him, spreading out like a thick carpet, hiding the bodies of the enemy. He found one and rolled it over. The moonlight filtered through a break in the canopy to reveal a dark stain on the man's chest and a ragged hole just above the right eye.

From there Bromhead worked his way to the mortar tube and found several rounds stacked near it. He figured that the enemy were setting it up to drop more rounds on the village, rather than breaking it down to escape.

Out of the corner of his eye, Bromhead discerned movement. It was Gilman. He stopped, stooped, and then a flash of reflected moonlight from a knife blade. There was a rustling on the ground, but no other sound. Gilman stood and moved closer to Bromhead.

"What's going on?" asked Bromhead.

"Enemy soldier expired due to his wounds."

"Shit!" exploded Bromhead. "What the hell did you knife him for? A prisoner we can interrogate, not a corpse."

"He was too shot up to move and wasn't going to last much longer anyway. Couldn't see the point in letting him die taking a shot at one of us."

"There was a third man. Find him."

"Already have. He's dead, too. Took a couple of bullets in the chest. That stopped him."

"Why didn't you use grenades?"

Gilman shook his head. "I didn't want to damage the tube. I figured we could use it and I thought I could take them all with a single burst."

"Okay," said Bromhead, sighing in exasperation. "Gather the weapons, equipment and any documents you can find. I'll break down the tube and we'll add all this to our supplies."

Both froze at the sound of a snapping twig. Bromhead pointed to the right and then moved to the left as Gilman began sliding toward the trees. Bromhead found cover, listened and then began easing his way back to the right. There was a thud, like a body hitting the soft ground and Bromhead wondered if Gilman had found another enemy. Then there was a giggle that someone tried to suppress.

Bromhead crouched, heard the laughter again, and moved toward it. He found one of the villagers, a crossbow clutched in his hand. At Bromhead's approach, the man looked up, tried to get to his feet and toppled to his side. He continued to laugh.

"What'll we do?" asked Gilman, who had appeared suddenly.

"Collect the gear, then get the fuck out of here."

"You think there's more of them? I mean the VC."

"No. I think it was one team sent out for harassment. We'll have to talk to the headman and see how often this happens. I hope it's a coincidence and not because some smartass VC figured we were in the area. If they know we're here already, we're fucked."

"Right."

"Let's break down the tube," said Bromhead, "and get out of here."

"Right," repeated Gilman.

They returned to the village quickly, the giggling man following them and making enough noise to wake everyone in the village, except that the majority of them were drunk instead of asleep. As they entered, Bromhead directed the man to the rest of his sleeping friends, most of whom had slept through the mortar attack. Then Gilman and Bromhead headed for the weapons hootch.

Hansen was alone inside, pawing through a canvas bag that had a red cross on it.

"Any wounded out there?" inquired Bromhead.

"No, sir. Mortars landed at the edge of the village. One dropped near here and another on the far side. Might have been someone hurt if they hadn't had the party."

"Where's Jane Lucas?"

"She took off right after you left. Said she was going to check on the children, but none of them were injured." Hansen closed the bag. "Funny how they all slept through it."

"Given the fact that the majority were drunk out of their skulls, I'm not surprised."

Hansen set the bag down and stood. "What do you think of that lady? Running around here dressed like that. I mean, showing her tits and going native like that."

"She's some kind of a scientist." Bromhead could have told Hansen that she was an anthropologist, but didn't want to complicate the matter. He knew something of their methods, and given that, he wasn't surprised by her.

"Yeah, well, she should still cover herself. It's not right."

"It may not be right," said Bromhead, smiling, "but it's not such a bad idea."

"Yes, sir," said Hansen, unconvinced.

Gilman entered at that point. "Are we going to put out a guard detail tonight?"

Bromhead rubbed a hand across the back of his neck, surprised at how wet it was. He wiped the perspiration on his sweat-stained fatigues. "I think we're in the clear for tonight. The important thing was that the mortar team wasn't moving the tube. If this had been a response to our presence, I think they would have had more teams, including a security unit. I suspect Charlie and his friends don't know we're here."

"But when the mortar crew doesn't return, he's going to suspect something," said Gilman.

"That point is debatable, too," said Bromhead. "But we'll assume it's correct. For the rest of tonight, I want us to form a roving guard. Two hours apiece, moving inside the trees where we'll be hard to find, but can hear or see the enemy if they approach. Tomorrow, the second thing we do is work out a schedule for guard duty."

Gilman sat on the floor and punched the magazine release on his M-1 carbine. He worked the bolt to eject the chambered round and then watched as it rolled between the cracks in the floor and disappeared. He pulled a full magazine from his pouch and slapped it into the well. He leaned over toward a box of ammo and extracted enough to refill the used magazine.

"I'll take the first shift, if no one objects," said Gilman.

"Suit yourself." Bromhead shrugged. "I guess I'll catch some sleep in that case. Hansen, you want the next shift or the last?"

"I'll take the next one."

"You got it." Bromhead was silent for a moment, watching the men with him. He moved to one corner of the hootch with his sleeping bag. "After tonight we'll spread out. Don't want to give the enemy all of us with one round. Any ideas you come up with, let me know. Now, I'm going to try to catch some shut-eye.''

Gilman, holding his weapon in his left hand, ducked out the door, stopped and glanced back. ''Captain, there's a lady here to see you.''

Bromhead groaned and shook his head. ''By all means,'' he said, ''send her in.''

Lucas entered, her face a mask. She wiped a hand through her hair, whipping it out of her eyes as she stared straight at Bromhead. ''I told you this was going to happen. I told you, but you wouldn't listen.''

''I know what you said,'' responded Bromhead evenly, ''but I don't think the attack was our fault. We'll know more about it in the morning.''

''This hasn't happened before.'' She moved forward, facing him, her hands on her hips. There was dirt streaked across one shoulder and on her stomach. Her hair hung loose, tangled and dirty.

''Jane,'' he said patiently, ''there is no way the attack can be blamed on us. It takes time to get men into position to launch a mortar attack. It had to be planned days in advance and is a coincidence that it came tonight.''

''Says you.''

''Okay, before we reduce this to a completely childish level, let me say this. We'll ask tomorrow. If this sort of thing has happened before, we'll know that it wasn't our fault. Besides, you saw how ineffective it was. Charlie would never have tipped his hand in such an amateurish fashion.'' He wiped a hand across his forehead and then stared at the sweat on his fingers. It wasn't that hot now, but he was sweating. He couldn't believe he was that upset by the debate with Lucas.

''Again, that is your opinion.''

''That doesn't change the facts. It only underscores the need for our help.''

"If you had any respect for these people, if you cared for them, you'd be gone in the morning." She spun and vanished into the night.

Bromhead sat there, staring at the door for several minutes. Then he looked at Hansen, who was lying on his side trying to get some sleep. "You know," he said, "I think she might be right."

"No, sir," said Hansen, without turning. "She thinks she's right, but she doesn't understand the ways of the world. She doesn't understand that people will not leave others alone when they can dominate them."

Bromhead turned down the lantern until it was barely glowing. He lay back, his hands locked under his head, and stared into the thatch above him. Hansen was right. She didn't understand.

5

THE MEO VILLAGE, LAOS

Bromhead was up with the sun but the villagers weren't. They were still scattered around the village, sleeping on the ground, under the hootches and behind the fences. A few of the women were awake and had started cooking fires under black pots holding water. The children were sitting in the doorways of their hootches, waiting for the adults to tell them what to do. None of them were making any noise.

After completing one circuit, Bromhead returned to the weapons hootch. He looked inside and saw Gilman sprawled in one corner, an arm over his eyes, snoring. Hansen was sitting quietly to one side, cleaning the grease from one of the M-1 carbines.

"Wake Gilman up," said Bromhead. "I'll see about getting some hot water for coffee."

"I'm awake," came a muffled voice from Gilman's direction.

"Hand me the canteen cups," said Bromhead, ignoring Gilman.

As he walked through the village toward one of the cooking fires, he found the headman sitting on the ground, his head down as if staring at the ground between his legs. When he heard Bromhead, he looked up and smiled weakly.

"When you have had your breakfast," said Bromhead, "please come by our hootch so that we can begin."

The man nodded carefully, as if afraid his head would fall off.

Bromhead laughed and headed toward the smoke. He had to check two pots before he found one with boiling water. It wasn't as easy getting some as he had thought. Most of the villagers didn't speak French but he finally, through gestures and sign language, conveyed his desire. The woman nodded happily, as if it was an honor to share her water with him.

Back at the weapons hootch, Bromhead sat cross-legged on the floor and poured the contents of a small, brown envelope into his cup. The coffee grounds sank immediately. He used a white plastic spoon to stir it, swirling the water, but the coffee refused to dissolve.

"I wonder who is responsible for buying this shit." Bromhead spoke to no one in particular, shaking his head.

"Some congressman who has an instant coffee manufacturing plant in his home district," said Hansen. "He gets the owner a government contract to produce it, the owner hires the local population to work in the local factory who in turn vote to keep the congressman in office, and the product is sent to military bases thousands of miles away. So who cares if it's not the best coffee. Who's going to know?"

Bromhead set the cup down and looked at the mud on the bottom. "You'd think that the people would take pride in their work. You'd think they'd want to give their soldiers the best product they could."

"Yes," said Hansen, "that's what you'd think."

"What happened to Gilman?"

At that moment Gilman appeared, clapping his hands against his arms as if he was cold. "I needed to piss," he said.

He then sat and asked, "That the coffee?" in a voice that was gravelly and too loud.

"In theory." Bromhead's face was serious.

"Well, I'll take a cup anyway." He blew on it, took a small sip and made a face. "Man, that's shitty. What is it? Some kind of local brew?"

"Nah," said Bromhead. "This is the good stuff manufactured in the U.S. of A. for the fighting men. It's the best there is."

"Thanks," said Gilman.

Bromhead changed the subject. "I think one of the first things we should do is find the mortar site, check it in the daylight and then bury the bodies. Two reasons for that. One is to make it harder for the enemy to find them. Maybe they'll think the men defected. And two, we can prevent disease."

A noise at the door attracted Bromhead's attention. The headman stood there waiting for permission to enter. Bromhead waved him in and gestured at the floor. When he was seated, Bromhead said, "Good morning, Colonel."

The headman nodded and then snapped his head up. "Colonel?"

"Yes," said Bromhead. "We shall organize strike companies in your village and you will, of course, command them. We'll draw the officers from the men you think will be responsible enough for the task."

"Yes, yes," said the man. "Colonel Beu. Yes, I like that."

"Now, Colonel Beu," said Bromhead, "might I suggest that you give Major Gilman a list of the men you'd like to see trained in the first company. These should be men who've had some training. Know something about the military."

"Then we kill Communists?" asked Beu.

"Just as soon as we have things organized, yes, we'll kill Communists."

IT HAD TAKEN GERBER and Fetterman most of the afternoon and part of the morning to learn the identity of the man they needed to see. They had circulated MACV Headquarters, buttonholing everyone who might have had the slightest knowledge of Bromhead's mission. Finally a platoon sergeant who claimed to be part of the Special Forces and who was wearing jump wings told them they should talk to Colonel Petersen.

They finally got to Petersen about midmorning. They pushed past the clerk who sat in the outer office typing on what looked like a brand new IBM typewriter. He leaped to protest, but neither Gerber nor Fetterman paused.

Inside the inner office, they found Petersen lying on a couch, a copy of *Stars and Stripes* over his head. The interior of the office was dark, the blinds drawn. A massive, wooden desk with a green blotter on it sat near the center of the room, a brown leather judge's chair behind it. Two similar high-backed chairs faced the desk. There was a conversation area in the corner, which contained the couch where Petersen slept. A smaller, two-person couch flanked that, and a square, dark, coffee table rested in front of them. The walls were paneled and the obligatory weapons of the Saigon chairborne commandos hung on the walls. There was even a Russian RPD hanging there.

"You think we should wake him?" asked Fetterman in a normal tone of voice.

"No. He's probably worn out from fighting communism in the officers' clubs all over Southeast Asia. We'll just sit quietly and wait."

Petersen pulled the paper from his face. He sat up, rubbed his eyes and stared at Gerber and Fetterman. As he dropped the paper to the floor he demanded, "Who are you clowns and how in the hell did you get in here?"

"We're Captain Gerber and Sergeant Fetterman." Gerber decided to take a seat. "We just walked in. We have a couple of questions and then we'll go."

Petersen sat quietly for a moment, as if he couldn't believe what had just happened. He reached up and fingered the collar of his uniform shirt as if fearing that the eagle sown there had fallen off. The look on his face told the visitors that he felt reassured his rank was visible. "Why don't you get out of here before you find yourselves in some real trouble?"

"Yes, sir," said Gerber, "just as soon as you tell us where Captain Bromhead was sent."

Petersen got to his feet and walked to his desk. His face was puffy and there was a red crease in the skin near his right ear where the edge of the couch had been pressed while he slept. He sat and rummaged through the drawers briefly. He took out a mirror to examine himself. He ran a hand through his hair, dropped the mirror into the drawer and then looked up, surprised.

"You men still here? I thought I told you to get out."

"Yes, sir," said Gerber, "as soon as we know where Captain Bromhead is."

"There a special reason you want to know this? You have orders from a higher headquarters, or are you here merely to make me angry?"

"No, sir. We just want to know about Captain Bromhead."

"Well, since you have no authority, I would suggest that you leave now."

Gerber looked at Fetterman, who had remained standing. "He's not going to cooperate, Tony."

"Sir." This time Fetterman addressed Petersen. "I know we're outside of normal channels, but you must understand that we have to watch out for the young captain. He's a babe in the woods and we want to make sure he's all right."

Petersen rubbed at an eye and then tugged at his ear. "Why this interest in Bromhead?"

"Used to be my exec," said Gerber. "He's a damned good man but he's out of touch with us."

"I assure you that he's safe. He's operating a covert mission for us here and will be out of touch for quite a while, I'm afraid."

"We understand that, sir," said Gerber. "We're not going to talk out of turn. We just want to know where he is."

"There's nothing you can do for him." Petersen took a folder from his desk and opened it.

Neither Gerber nor Fetterman moved. Finally Gerber spoke. "Our speculation leads us to a number of conclusions." He remained quiet for a moment and then continued. "He's obviously operating either in Cambodia or Laos. That would mean, at the very least, a limited CIA connection, although our case officer claims to know nothing about it."

"Captain," snapped Petersen, looking up from his folder, "such speculations can lead you into a great deal of trouble. Now why don't you and your sergeant leave?"

"Of course, we have your name, too, and you have inadvertently told us that you know something about this..."

"Are you threatening me?"

"Oh no, sir," said Fetterman. "We'd never do that. We're only suggesting that we'll need to take our inquiries elsewhere and some facts may leak. If we had the information, we could go quietly about our business."

Petersen stared at Fetterman for several long seconds. The colonel seemed to be making up his mind. Finally he said, "It's against my better judgment to say a word, but you two have been around long enough to know the score. I doubt you'd do anything that would leak information, because if I did believe that, I'd have you both up on charges."

"Yes, sir," said Gerber. "We're just trying to look out for one of our boys."

"None of this goes beyond this room. That's it. I find out you've talked to anyone about anything, the shit hits the fan. Understood?"

Both Fetterman and Gerber nodded.

"Captain Bromhead and a small team are in a little village in Laos training a couple of strike companies to interdict the Ho Chi Minh Trail."

Gerber stood and pulled a small map from his pocket. "Exactly where?"

Petersen looked annoyed, grabbed the map and stabbed a finger at it. "Here."

"Thank you, sir." Gerber folded his map. "Sorry to have bothered you."

"Remember what I told you," warned Petersen.

"Yes, sir," said Gerber as he and Fetterman retreated.

In the corridor, Fetterman turned to the captain. "Now what?"

"We get assigned to one of the Special Forces camps on the Vietnamese side of the border where we'll be in a position to offer help if Johnnie needs it."

"You mean Jack?"

"Yeah. Jack."

IT TOOK THEM AN HOUR to work their way to the mortar site using the proper military procedures. Bromhead and Gilman didn't give many instructions because they wanted to observe and find out how much the locals knew. The villagers, realizing that it was a test of some kind, slipped into their military roles with ease. They knew about patrol procedure and noise discipline, and although they were hung over from the night of celebration, no one let on that he was sick.

Bromhead and Gilman brought up the rear. Gilman surprised Bromhead by twice slipping into the jungle to relieve himself, claiming it was a result of the heavy drinking the night before. But since he did it in a military fashion, being careful to make no noise and leave no sign, Bromhead gave it no further thought.

They found nothing at the mortar site that would prove useful. The dead men were lying where they had fallen. Beu danced around them, firing kicks at the corpses. He wanted to cut off the ears, noses, and fingers, but Bromhead refused, claiming that his men had killed them so it was his right to choose to mutilate the bodies or not mutilate them as they saw fit. Beu saw the wisdom of that and ordered his men to help bury them.

Once they were back in the village, Beu gathered the fifteen men who had worked with the French and had them standing in a line outside the weapons hootch. Bromhead inspected them, made a few comments in French that were translated into Meo by Beu or Gilman, who used the skills he had learned in the language school.

Bromhead explained what they wanted to do. He ducked into the hootch and returned with one of the AK-47s and handed it to Beu. Bromhead told the men where they had gotten it, and it was the first of many weapons that would be taken from the Communists as trophies and signs of victory. Naturally the men could keep any weapons they captured, but they couldn't jeopardize the mission to take weapons. If someone did, then he forfeited his right to the weapon.

Hansen appeared and pulled a number of boxes out of the hootch. He arranged them on the ground and opened them. Bromhead told the men that these were their uniforms. Each man was responsible for the condition of his uniform. He was to keep it clean and in good condition.

The men started to swarm forward, but Bromhead halted them with a single, shouted command. Since there were enough uniforms, he would tolerate no mob action. They had to form a line and he and Hansen would hand out the clothes. Each man would give Hansen his name.

When the uniforms were issued, Bromhead had the men return to their own hootches for their weapons. They returned carrying machetes or crossbows and three of them had old rifles that had been cared for lovingly. The blueing was wearing off the barrels and the stocks were worn smooth, but it was obvious that the weapons would fire. If there had been any ammunition for them.

By the time Bromhead and Gilman had finished examining everything, it was nearly lunchtime. Bromhead told Beu to have the men break for lunch and he would expect them back in an hour. Training would begin in the afternoon.

Bromhead and his men retreated to their hootch for lunch. Inside, Hansen handed out the C-ration boxes and then sat down to eat.

Bromhead opened a can of boned chicken with a P-38 can opener. "After lunch I'm going to take Beu and four of his men on patrol. Gilman, you'll go with me. We'll sweep to the east, toward the Ho Chi Minh Trail. Hansen, you stay here and begin the training."

"If you don't mind a suggestion, sir," said Gilman. "Let me stay here. I can get the men started on creating a line of defense. Bunkers at the four corners and locate the spots for others. With enough people working on it, we'll have a good start by nightfall. And that'll give Hansen a chance to get out in the field finally."

Bromhead dug at the boned chicken with the white plastic spoon, then salted the food liberally. It was the only way to make the chicken palatable. He took a bite, chewed and swallowed. "I guess that makes sense."

"After we return, sir," said Hansen, "I can work on a few more of the weapons. Clean them up."

"No," said Bromhead. "I want you to have one available for Beu and one each for the company commanders when they're selected, but I think the others should clean their own. It'll be good training for them."

Bromhead finished his chicken, opened a can of bread and pulled it apart. There was a thin tin of jelly and Bromhead opened it. It was runny, but it was jelly. Bromhead dumped it on the bread and ate that. The last thing he opened was a can of fruit cocktail. When he finished eating, he jammed the empty cans back into the box. He held up the pack of cigarettes that came with the meal. "Either of you smoke these?"

"No, sir."

"Okay, let's collect them all and use them as bribes for the men."

"Say, sir," said Gilman, "you seen anything of that Lucas woman today?"

"No, but she's around though. You can bet on that."

Gilman nodded his agreement and then excused himself because he felt an uncontrollable urge to urinate.

IT TOOK NO TIME to organize the patrol. Bromhead and Hansen, both carrying M-1 carbines and several grenades, told Beu to get his best men and choose four of them for the mission, but to exclude the men who had gone out in the morning. Once those men were chosen, and Beu had assured them that each of the men knew how to use a rifle, the equipment was issued.

Bromhead outlined the mission in French, with Gilman standing by to translate anything that Bromhead couldn't get across. It was a simple recon through the jungle in the vicinity of the village. They were going to see if there was anything or anyone around that suggested the enemy, meaning the Pathet Lao, Vietcong and North Vietnamese. The equipment would be limited to a carbine, a knife, canteens on a pistol belt with a first-aid kit, and little else. No sense carrying things in the heat of the afternoon if it could be avoided.

Then Gilman split off to take charge of the working party, showing them where the bunkers would go. Bromhead watched him for a moment and, satisfied with that aspect of the mission, took the point with Beu.

As they moved across the grassy plain to the jungle, Bromhead spoke to the headman. "Normally we wouldn't go on the patrols. We'd send them out to learn what was happening around here, having them report to us, but the circumstances dictate that we make the initial recon."

"It is just as the last white men said," replied Beu. "They told us many of the things that you tell us."

At the edge of the jungle, Bromhead halted for a moment. The men had spread out in a military formation, one man directly behind the man in front of him, separated by five or six yards. Each man held his weapon in his hands, his finger not on the trigger but on the trigger guard. It indicated that the men had been well trained and that their training was coming back to them. It also meant that Bromhead's program could proceed faster than he had anticipated.

They entered the jungle, a green hothouse. The vegetation on the ground was sparse here and allowed them to move rapidly. Bromhead touched the smooth trunk of a teak, surprised to find it covered with moisture. The ground under his feet was soft, giving with each step, and then springing back as the pressure was removed.

Water dripped from the broad leaves of the bushes and as the men rubbed against them, splattered their uniforms. In minutes it was as if they were walking through a steam bath wrapped in damp towels. And the wetness didn't provide relief from the heat. The humidity kept the sweat and water from evaporating. It made the patrol more miserable.

By the time they had been on the move for thirty minutes, Bromhead was ready to call it off. His mouth felt stuffed with cotton and hung open. His muscles ached, burning like red hot wires stretched across his shoulders and shoved into his arms and legs, but he couldn't call a halt yet. It would show weakness to the villagers and that was the last thing he wanted to do.

When Beu looked at him, Bromhead closed his mouth and smiled weakly. He pointed to the right, where there was an outcropping of rock barely visible through the veil of green. Beu turned toward it and when he reached it, fell into a depression where he could rest.

As the men approached, he pointed and was pleased to see that they understood what he wanted. They formed a loose circle where each man could watch the man on his right and left. They faced outward, their weapons ready. Then, as if some unheard command had been spoken, every other man set his rifle down, careful to keep the operating rod out of the dirt. They drank the water from their canteens in short sips, poured some of it over their heads, letting their soft caps absorb it, and then returned the canteens to their canvas covers. As they picked up their weapons, the other men went through the procedure.

Bromhead slipped close to Beu. "Your men are very good in the jungle," the American whispered.

"We slip up on the Communists and cut their throats. They never know what hit them."

"In time that is exactly what we'll do."

"I bring best men to show you. These be my officers."

"Good choices, every one," said Bromhead. "I'm very pleased with them."

"We go kill Communists then. We get even with them for chasing us."

"Soon. Very soon."

Beu nodded grimly, his knuckles turning white where he gripped the M-1 carbine. It was as if the answer didn't please him.

"Let's swing to the south now," said Bromhead. "I think everyone has had enough rest."

Beu got to his feet and raised his hand over his head. The men stood and waited. The silent command was just another proof of their training. Someone had worked long and hard with these men, not only teaching them the techniques, but showing them that it worked better than anything else.

This time Bromhead strained to catch the sounds of the men moving through the jungle. But all he heard were the animals in the trees, the birds flapping and the chirps of insects on the ground. He could hear nothing that would indicate a party of men was near. He stopped once, heard a monkey overhead and saw the beast swinging from tree to tree, squawking as it went, as if alerting its fellows. It disappeared quickly.

Suddenly, ahead of him, Bromhead heard the babble of voices. Two or tree men talking to one another. None of the voices was loud and the talk didn't seem to be a conversation. It sounded more like orders being given.

Bromhead raised his arm to halt the patrol. Over his shoulder, he saw the men take up positions facing in opposite directions so that no one could sneak up on them. When they were set, Bromhead touched Beu on the shoulder, then pointed to the front. Together they worked their way toward the sound, moving slowly, avoiding the twig that might snap or the bush that might rustle.

It took ten minutes to move twenty yards. The voices were sporadic, coming quietly. Bromhead dropped flat once and felt the damp of the ground soak through his uniform. As he crawled forward, he felt mud and slime stain his clothes and coat his hands. He ignored it, his attention focused on the people in front of him.

He came to a large log lying at a slight angle where its thick branches had been caught by another tree. He slipped under it and looked out into a tiny clearing bordered by a brook. Sunlight danced on the water's surface, splintering the light and reflecting it.

Seated around a small fire were six men wearing the green uniforms of the NVA, ill-fitting fatigues that held no insignia. Each of the men had a pith helmet with a red star on it and each wore a chest pouch that held spare magazines for their weapons. One man, who was probably an officer, had a holster holding a Makarov pistol. The enlisted weapons, AK-47s, were stacked near them. Now that Bromhead could see the fire, he caught a whiff of the smoke, but couldn't see it rising. He noticed that the soldiers had built a canopy over the fire, which helped to disperse the smoke. It was a layered affair that caused the smoke to dissipate.

Beu crawled up beside him, his weapon ready. He aimed it and slipped off the safety. Bromhead put a hand on the barrel and shook his head. He held his hand up, indicating to Beu that they should wait. He then moved backward, his eyes on the enemy soldiers. Before they attacked the group, Bromhead wanted his whole force in position.

At that moment a snapping sound to the right made Bromhead look up. Standing over him, his hand on his fly was an NVA soldier, a bewildered look on his face. His jaw dropped and he reached for his pistol.

Bromhead pushed himself onto his back, swinging up his M-1 toward the man. Before Bromhead could fire, there was a single shot behind him and the enemy's face disintegrated into a crimson pulp. His hand spasmed, jerking his weapon from his holster and dropping it into the jungle.

From the clearing came a shout. Shooting broke out around him. Bromhead heard his men running forward and throwing themselves to the ground. He spun, scrambled to his feet and leaped for the fallen tree moments before a burst of AK fire slammed into it, making it shudder. Bark and wood splintered, flying all around him. Bromhead aimed over the top. He fired rapidly, jerking at the trigger in his haste.

One of the enemy was hit, spinning to the right. He fell to one knee and reached out for the rifle he had dropped. Bromhead fired again. The round thudded almost dead center into the enemy's chest. The man flipped back, his legs doubling under him.

Two men sprang up, AKs in their hands, firing on full automatic. The bullets ripped through the jungle, snapping at the leaves and bushes. One man went to the right and the other left, trying to outflank Bromhead.

Bromhead turned, his rifle sights on one of them. He pulled the trigger, missed and fired again. The bolt locked back as the man dived into the vegetation. Bromhead spun, his back to the tree and hit the magazine release. As the spent magazine fell free, Bromhead grabbed another, slammed it home and jerked at the bolt. With a round chambered, Bromhead dropped to the ground, searching for the enemy.

Around him the others were firing now, a rippling noise of M-1 carbines and AK-47s. There were bursts and lulls as the men searched for each other in the jungle. There was a grunt and a shot and then more silence. Bromhead was afraid to move because he didn't know where his men were now. They had obviously advanced toward the edge of the clearing.

Firing broke out on the right, unseen in the mist rising from the jungle floor and the half-light created by the dense vegetation. Bromhead turned and crawled under the log. In the patches of light in the clearing, he saw the bodies of three men. He pulled his gaze away from them, watching the jungle, searching for the NVA.

He caught movement at the very edge, aimed, but didn't fire because he didn't know who it was. A moment later one of

Beu's men slid into view. Then, behind him, another shadow approached. Bromhead couldn't see clearly, but the shape of the weapon was wrong. As the man closed with the first, Bromhead pulled the trigger. There was a shout of pain as the man jumped sideways into the jungle.

Beu's man leaped into the clearing, rolled and came up firing at the enemy soldier Bromhead had hit. Then, his weapon empty, he jumped back for cover among the trees.

Bromhead crawled out from under the log and stood, the log to his back. He scanned the jungle and saw no more movement. The firing had died away, only the distant echoes resounding and fading in the distance. Bromhead took a hesitant step forward, heard a crash of vegetation to his right. He spun in time to see the NVA soldier launch himself. He hit Bromhead in the chest, bowling him over.

Bromhead rolled with the blow, losing his rifle. The man scrambled forward, sitting on Bromhead's chest. In his hand he grasped a knife, the blade glittering. Bromhead's hand shot out to grab the wrist. He locked his elbow as the knife came plunging toward his chest. At the same moment, Bromhead swung with his right hand. The punch slammed into his adversary's neck just under the jawbone. A spray of spittle flew out of the Oriental's mouth as he grunted and rolled to his right.

Bromhead grabbed at his holster. His pistol cleared the leather, and he came up on one arm and fired. The first round hit the enemy in the side with a loud, wet smack. He grunted in surprise and pain. Bromhead fired again and the man jerked upright, as if trying to sit. Bromhead's third shot struck him in the face, ripping off his lower jaw, leaving a dripping, gaping red wound as the man died.

From the other side of the clearing came the chattering of an AK-47. That was answered by two M-1 carbines being fired semiautomatically. An instant later Hansen emerged. He crossed the clearing, ignoring the dead enemy.

"At least one of them got away. Had too much of a lead on us. I think we got the other."

Bromhead turned to Beu. "Check the bodies. Pick up the weapons." Then he told Hansen, "Don't run across the battlefield until we've cleared it."

"Those guys are dead."

"You don't know that. Could be some brave suicide lying in wait for a nice fat target to get into range. Now, why didn't you follow the enemy?"

"Too far ahead of us. One guy dropped back to shoot while the other ran. I didn't want to get us spread too thin."

"Good thinking."

"Thank you, sir."

"Anyone hurt? You see any of our men go down?"

Hansen shook his head. "No. I've seen them all. Beu was talking to one of them. We got through this in good shape."

"That's good. Now, help check the bodies. Grab anything you think will be useful to us, but don't leave anything for the enemy to recover. And take one of the weapons as a souvenir." He rubbed a hand over his face, wiping away the sweat.

"No thanks," said Hansen. "I don't want one."

Bromhead shook his head. "Doesn't matter. You take one as a souvenir. Maybe we can convince these guys that the weapons make better trophies than ears and fingers."

"Oh."

Bromhead crouched by the man he had shot with his pistol. The sight of the corpse almost made him sick. He didn't like the sight of broken human bodies. The act of killing the man didn't bother him because that was expected. Since he had selected an armed force for his career, he had expected to be placed in a position to have to kill another human and had long ago made his peace with himself. He didn't like the act of killing, and regretted having to do it, but he preferred that it was the enemy lying dead in the dirt, not himself. It wasn't something he wanted to try. But sometimes the sight of the broken bodies, arms blown off or stomachs ripped open or heads smashed with the brains leaking out, bothered him. He would have preferred the clean, sterile wounds often portrayed by Hollywood. But real battle and real death were never quite that clean.

"We've got everything," said Hansen. "Except from this guy."

Bromhead looked up. "Get the men formed and ready to move out. I'll take care of this guy."

Trying to keep his eyes off the mess that had been the man's face, Bromhead patted the pockets and extracted a wallet. He put it in his own pocket. He took the weapons, the knife and the canteen and felt the pants pockets. He pulled out a couple of coins and wondered about the wisdom of running around the jungle with loose change. Of course, this was Laos and the NVA didn't expect trouble in Laos.

Bromhead got to his feet and looked at his men. They stood in formation at the edge of the clearing in the shade, away from the burning rays of the sun. All eyes were on him, and he wished their discipline was a little better.

He pointed at Beu and said in French, "Let's head back to the village. Keep the pace steady, but not too fast. I'll bring up the rear."

Beu nodded and waved a hand over his head.

As the patrol moved out, Bromhead took a final look at the battlefield. Not much of a firefight. Probably lasted less than five minutes, but to the men who had died, it was the most important one they would ever fight in. Too bad no one would ever hear about it. He turned and followed his men into the jungle on their way home.

6

THE MEO VILLAGE, LAOS

While Bromhead and Hansen were wandering around the jungle, Gilman was standing in the center of the village, trying to explain the importance of building bunkers. The men couldn't see the point of building them when it was easier to fade away in the jungle. They didn't want to fight from holes in the ground, but wanted to be out in the open where they could move around, and where their ancestors could see them.

Gilman explained it to them at length and then realized what was happening. It wasn't that the men didn't understand what he was talking about. They didn't think soldiers should build bunkers. Building bunkers was something that the men who were not worthy of being soldiers should do. Soldiers would fight in them, not build them.

Finally Gilman said, "But you are the men who will be fighting in them. Do you want to trust someone with the knowledge you have gained by building your fighting position? Would you let that man handle your weapon, clean it and maintain it? Isn't it the soldier's duty to take care of his weapon? Isn't a soldier's duty to build his own bunker?"

They saw the logic of the argument and finally agreed. Gilman, weary from the argument, dragged a couple of shovels from the weapons hootch, tossed three axes out and then pushed out several bundles of empty sandbags. He assigned men to each of the tools and then led them to the corner of the village.

"Here," he said, "we'll build our first bunker."

With his knife, he sharpened a stick and used it to draw a square on the ground. He pointed at it and was tempted to tell them that their dirt was in his hole, but was sure the joke would be lost on them. Instead he showed them how to dig the hole with straight walls, how to fill and stack the sandbags. Then he got out of the way. The men with the axes were instructed to get some logs about six feet long and a foot thick. They would be used to reinforce the bunker and to build the roof.

As he moved back to watch the progress, surprised that the men needed so little supervision once convinced the task wasn't beneath them, Jane Lucas appeared. She was dressed in the native costume of a brightly colored cloth knotted around the waist. It hung to her knee on one side but left her thigh bare on the other. She wore sandals and nothing else.

"Good afternoon." Gilman averted his eyes from her breasts. Beads of perspiration glistened on her face and ran down her chest. When she didn't respond in English, he greeted her in the Meo's language.

She snapped around as if she had been shot, her gaze unwavering. "You speak the language?"

"Yes, ma'am. After a fashion. I'm not real proficient on all the tenses and some of the words, with their slight changes in inflection, throw me off."

"I'm surprised. I heard your commander speaking his high school French, but I didn't know that any of you were conversant in Meo."

Gilman grinned at her and asked in the native tongue, "What brings you out here this afternoon?"

She pointed at the work party and asked, in English, "What are you doing?"

"Constructing the beginnings of a defensive system. If Charlie, or rather the Communists, decide to hit this village, we want to be ready for him."

"And if you weren't here, none of this would be necessary," she said angrily.

"I'm not sure you're right on that one, ma'am," said Gilman.

"I am. There have been no attacks on us until you arrived. Then, all of a sudden, someone starts dropping bombs on us last night."

"Colonel Bromhead seems to think that you would've been mortared last night even if we hadn't shown up. The bad guys got into position too fast for us to be the cause."

"Well, if the colonel says so, then it must be right," she said sarcastically.

"Ask Beu if they've ever been mortared before. I think you'll find that it's not that rare an occurrence. I've seen a couple of people running around here with scars that suggest that all has not been peaceful."

"You all think alike," said Lucas, "I'll give you that. It's like talking to your commander. Don't care about anything but doing your job, no matter who gets in the way."

Gilman looked at her and then turned back to watch the men working. He wiped the sweat from his face with his sleeve. "And people like you don't think anyone else knows what he's doing. There is the possibility that we do know what we're doing here."

"Of course," she said. "You'd believe that, too."

"If I didn't, I wouldn't be here. You know, if the North Vietnamese win in the South, there's nothing to keep them from moving into Laos and Cambodia. And when they do, they're going to eliminate everyone who ever fought them or spoke out against them or had any kind of education. It won't matter to them. They'll just round them up and kill them.''

"And you believe that?"

Gilman looked at her, stared at her bare breasts as if trying to embarrass her. He became aware of a burning at his crotch. "Nothing I can say would change your mind. You have all the answers because the Communists are such wonderful people they would never lie and they certainly wouldn't hurt anyone."

"I didn't say that, but I don't think they're the evil that you people claim they are."

"Look, I have a lot of work to do here. The colonel said not to be rude to you, so if you'll forgive me, I'll get back to my work." He stepped closer to the hole and crouched at the edge. He pretended to inspect it, said something to the men working in it and then turned. Lucas was walking toward the center of the village. He watched her for a moment, wondering if she was going to cause them problems. Suddenly he broke into a run toward the jungle. The burning had become an overpowering pain and he had to relieve himself quickly.

BROMHEAD AND HIS PATROL arrived at the village about an hour before dark. They halted at the tree line, just inside the jungle, to observe the men working at the edge of the village. Gilman had taken off his fatigue shirt and was standing there bare-chested, his ID tags tossed over his shoulder. All Bromhead could see was the chain around his neck.

The work was progressing well. One bunker had been completed. It was a low affair, sticking only two feet above the ground, hidden under a layer of sandbags. It was barely visible over the grass and Bromhead realized that they were going to have to burn off the field.

As they entered the clearing, Gilman caught movement out of the corner of his eye. He jerked to the right to snare his weapon and then saw Bromhead. He held up a hand and waved.

Bromhead turned to Beu. "Tell the men we'll have a weapons check in fifteen minutes. I want to see the weapons cleaned and oiled and ready for inspection. Anyone who needs help, see Major Hansen."

Hansen was about to protest the rank when he remembered that Bromhead had given him the brevet promotion.

"Follow me," said Hansen in English, moving toward the weapons hootch.

"Major Gilman," said Bromhead. "I need to have a word with you."

Gilman stepped away from the men working on the bunker and then laughed. Not one of them could speak English. "What do you need, sir?"

"We ran into a group of NVA and got into a firefight with them. Killed most of them, but at least one got away."

"Oh shit!" Gilman picked up his shirt and wiped his hands on it. He found his weapon, then spoke to the men, "You keep working here until the sun touches the horizon. Then you can go." He slipped the shirt on but didn't button it. The sweat on his shoulders and back soaked it quickly. "What are you planning to do?"

Bromhead turned, heading toward the weapons hootch. "Haven't figured it out yet."

"Wasn't Hansen's fault, was it?"

"No. He did quite well, as a matter of fact. Oh, he could have been a little sharper, but I can't complain. And the Meos are terrific. They know exactly what they're doing. If Beu can come up with another thirty of them, we've got our cadre. A good, experienced cadre."

"So what are you planning?" asked Gilman.

"Haven't thought about that, either. If we had gotten them all, we could figure on a week, maybe longer, before we had to worry about the enemy showing up. But someone got away and that cuts into our time.''

''Did he see you?''

''Who knows? Christ, Gilman, it was a firefight. I don't know who saw what.''

''Then at best we have forty-eight hours.''

''That's kind of what I thought,'' said Bromhead. ''If Beu has the men, we could hand out the weapons tomorrow, spend the day cleaning them and get an ambush out the next. Slow down the VC a little.''

Gilman stopped at the notched log and let Bromhead climb it first. Inside, they found Hansen and two of the men cleaning weapons, the parts scattered on the floor around them. Hansen looked up and grinned, then went back to work.

Bromhead unbuckled his pistol belt and dropped it to the floor. He moved to the stack of C-rations and pawed through them, searching for a can of peaches. When he found them, he sat down on the floor, used a P-38 to open them and drank the syrup. A hundred thoughts flashed through his mind. Plans for dealing with the coming of the NVA, the VC and the Pathet Lao. Things that needed to be done before the enemy arrived. He wondered if the ambush was a good idea. If it would buy them more time, then it was right. But it might also tip their hand.

Bromhead watched the men reassembling their weapons. They studied Hansen's movements and followed his lead, but they did it rapidly, demonstrating a knowledge of firearms. It wasn't something he expected to find in a primitive village in the Laotian mountains.

''That anthropologist lady visited me this afternoon,'' said Gilman.

''And told you to get out of the village.''

''No, sir. Suggested we were doing more harm than good, though.''

"I don't have time to worry about her. She's just one of those college liberals who believe in the ideal world and don't realize that the real world bears no resemblance."

"So what do we do?"

Bromhead continued to eat. He chewed and swallowed. "First, I'm going to finish my peaches. Second, we'll talk to Beu and see if he has the men we need."

"You want me to go out and see if I can find the man who got away?"

"No. It'll be dark in a few minutes and you'd never be able to find the trail at night. That gives him a good twelve-hour head start. We'll need all the help we can get here without worrying about a frightened enemy soldier."

"So when does all this start?" asked Gilman.

"First light tomorrow."

BEU HAD FORMED THE MEN into a straight line behind one of the new bunkers. Some of them wore the uniforms that had been issued the day before. Others stood in the early morning light in only a loincloth. All stood at attention, their eyes locked forward, waiting for Bromhead and his staff to arrive and give them their orders.

When he approached, Bromhead saluted Beu. "Good morning, Colonel."

Beau returned the salute and responded, "Good morning. I have the men ready."

"Yes, I see." Bromhead counted them. Forty-seven of them stood there. "All these men have had military experience?"

"Yes," said Beu. "All have training."

"All right. I want to get everyone into a uniform. Then we'll pass out the rifles. Each man will be responsible for cleaning his own weapon. When that's finished, we'll visit the range for a little target practice."

Beu nodded his agreement. Bromhead pulled him aside and spoke to him quietly, "But first we need to get some scouts out. You must select five of your very best men and send them out to look for the Communists. They must not kill them, only count them and bring the information back to us. They must be here tomorrow morning at the latest. Do you understand?"

"I understand."

"It's important that these men count the enemy soldiers and not shoot them. They cannot take their rifles, only their crossbows. They must dress in loincloths. They must be quiet and not be seen."

"The men will not like leaving their guns."

"It is something they must do. You tell them the rifles will be here when they return. The best we have, and the first weapons we capture, will be given to them. They must understand the importance of this. If they do it right, we will be able to kill many of the Communists."

Beu crouched and rocked back on his haunches, studying the problem. He picked up a twig and scribbled in the dirt with it. "This will be difficult."

"Only the very best men can do this. Once we find the enemy, they will lead us to him and we will kill many more of them." Bromhead smiled.

"I see what can be done." Beu stood and walked among the assembled men. He tapped five of them on the chest and pulled them out of the formation. He took them aside and spoke in low tones for several minutes. When he finished, he waved at Bromhead.

"The men understand."

"Tell them," said Bromhead, "that we want them to split up and circulate to the north and east of here. Look for the Communists but don't shoot at them."

Beau repeated the instructions and when he finished, Bromhead said, "I want to see them before they go. You have them come by the weapons hootch when they are ready."

Bromhead split the remaining men into two groups of twenty. One was given to Gilman who was instructed to take them to the weapons hootch and get them into uniform. Bromhead and Hansen took charge of the other group, most of whom were already in uniform, and marched them to the hootch. While Gilman was handing out the uniforms, Hansen distributed the weapons. Bromhead instructed them in the cleaning of the weapons while Beu translated into their own language. Gilman was left alone with his group, doing the same.

The whole morning was spent getting the weapons ready. The grease on some of them was so thick that it could be removed in handfuls. It took an hour just to get them ready to be cleaned. Bromhead led his group through the process slowly, showing them how to clean the grease by using rags. Once they were cleaned, they were oiled carefully and reassembled. Bromhead walked among his group, watching and pointing and assisting, checking the progress of the work. And as the day before, he saw that the men had been well trained by someone. They were attentive, listening to each of his instructions, and they were careful. No one left small parts out. No one inverted anything or inserted it backward.

The only interruption was when the five scouts arrived. Bromhead checked them closely to make sure they were carrying nothing that would help the enemy. He cautioned them again about getting back by the following morning, even if they didn't find the Communists. Then he sent them on their way. If one of them failed to return, Bromhead intended to order Beu to have his villagers flee because it would mean the Communists were on the way.

When the weapons were ready and checked, Bromhead issued magazines for them. He opened a crate of .30-caliber carbine ammunition and started the men loading the magazines. They kept at that until each man had five banana clips with thirty rounds apiece. For target practice, he issued each man two fifteen-round magazines and told them to load those.

By then it was time for lunch. Bromhead called a halt and was about to send the men to their hootches for an hour off when Beu invited him to eat the afternoon meal with him. Bromhead had looked forward to eating a C-ration lunch but didn't see how he could refuse. He let Beu lead him away.

The lunch was served on palm leaves by Beu's wives. One of them sat in the corner, watching the other two. One of them, a slender young woman, served the main course of monkey. The other, an older woman with a bad scar on her back, served snake and parrot and vegetables. She knelt near them, waiting for instructions from the other two women.

Bromhead studied the scar. It was a bullet hole that had hit her in the back above the shoulder blade and exited in the front, leaving an ugly, puckered wound. Her left arm did not work as well as it should and she held it at an awkward angle.

Halfway through the meal, Beu looked up and saw that Bromhead had finished most of his stew. Beu snapped his fingers at the woman. The first wife leaped from her place in the corner and slapped the woman. There was a burst of shouting as she hit the woman again and again.

Bromhead said, quickly, "That's not necessary."

Beu looked at Bromhead and grinned widely. "You like this woman?" he asked.

"She is a human being," responded Bromhead.

"Then you may have her."

"What do you mean, have her?" asked Bromhead. "She is one of your wives."

"I took her in because no other man would have her. With her crippled arm, she cannot carry a full load or do her share of the work. No other warrior wants her."

At first Bromhead was going to refuse. Then he remembered that the customs of the Meo were different. To refuse might be seen as a lack of feeling for the locals. He was pushed into a corner, having to accept the gift, even if the gift was a human being.

Bromhead nodded. "Then she must go to my hootch and wait for me there."

Beu grinned again and said something in rapid-fire Meo. The woman glanced at Bromhead but said nothing. She turned, ducked her way out of the hootch and disappeared.

When she was gone, the meal resumed with the number two wife serving alone. The atmosphere of hostility vanished when the crippled woman left.

After lunch Bromhead returned to the weapons hootch. The woman was inside, kneeling near Bromhead's gear, waiting for him. He told her to relax because he had nothing for her to do. Then he left for the south side of the village where his men had assembled for rifle practice.

Using boards ripped from the ammo crates and a marker pen, Bromhead created a number of bull's-eye targets and set them up about a hundred and fifty yards from his makeshift firing line. He explained what he had in mind, told the ten men on the firing line to shoot only at the target in front of him and to only fire five shots. They would inspect the targets afterward.

The afternoon was spent putting each group through the procedure, ten men at a time. Again Bromhead was surprised. Most of the men were good shots, many of them excellent. None of them had the habit of closing their eyes or firing high, which was the trouble with men who had never fired a rifle before. He selected the best of the shots as squad leaders and platoon sergeants. Beu choose two lieutenants as platoon leaders and Bromhead made Gilman the company commander.

By dusk he had his first-strike company, trained and ready for action. As they left the rifle range for the evening, the company dispersing into the village to join their families, Bromhead wondered just how good the training was. He hadn't trained them and hadn't expected to be this far along for weeks. He was relying on someone else's work, and although that work had been done well, Bromhead was a little worried about it. After all, he had only seen five or six of the men in combat, if the brief firefight in the jungle could be called combat. They had reacted well, had been disciplined, but that was a small group with everything breaking their way. A pitched battle against an equal force of NVA or VC could be a disaster.

He walked into the weapons hootch, set his carbine down and then sat on one of the unopened crates. The woman came to him and touched his arm. Bromhead looked at her and smiled. He told her that she didn't have to remain. Without a word, she crossed the hootch and sat near the stone platform that was the fireplace.

Bromhead wished he had a cold beer. He needed something to chill the throat and freeze the stomach. Instead he could only sit on the crate, his elbows on his knees, and stare at the floor. At best, there was some warm water in the canteen. He realized just how important the little things were. Cold beer, air-conditioning, a shower and a flush toilet. He could remember thinking about each of those sometime during the day.

If he wanted a bath to remove the grime and sweat, he would have to find a stream. If he wanted air-conditioning, he would have to wave a piece of cardboard in front of his face. But there was no beer, cold or otherwise. Only the local brew, lukewarm, that could blow off the top of the head in a matter of seconds.

Bromhead unbuttoned his sweat-soaked shirt and wiped his face with the damp ends. His entire uniform was soaked, as if he had just run through a heavy rain. If he changed it, the same thing would happen within minutes. After nightfall, the mountain air would cool but he still wouldn't be comfortable. There was absolutely nothing he could do about it except forget it and concentrate on something more important.

He heard a noise at the door and turned to see Jane Lucas standing there. She half-waved at him. "Mind if I come in?"

"Suit yourself."

Jane entered, surveyed the mess, and then noticed the woman at the far end of the hootch. The anthropologist looked at the open crates, the scattered packing paper, the cardboard boxes that had held ammunition. When she finished looking it all over, she said, "So it's true."

Bromhead looked up at her and realized that she was back in her safari outfit. He wondered why he found the costume more erotic than the bare-breasted native garb she sometimes wore. Then he wondered why he thought about it at all.

"What's true?" he asked, thinking about the softness of her skin as he had pulled her to the floor during the mortar attack. He remembered the texture of her skin, the dampness of it as he had tried to protect her, and found the thoughts exciting.

"That you're planning something big. The women are having some kind of death ritual, which means they think their men are going off to war."

Bromhead shook his head. "Now that's one thing I never thought about. The men and women preparing for battle with a funeral. Sure telegraphs the moves."

"Why?" she asked as she rubbed her hands on her thighs as if to dry them. "Why do you have to do this?"

"Jane, let me ask you a question. Have you talked to these people about their life before you arrived? Have you asked about the wounds some of them have?"

She moved closer to Bromhead and sat on the edge of an upturned crate. She glanced at the woman near the fireplace again. She put her hands on her bare knees and studied the floor between her feet. "Yes," she admitted. "I've talked to them and asked about the wounds."

"Then you have some idea of what is happening here. What has happened here."

"Yes. Some. But I know that your being here is endangering everyone else."

Bromhead turned his head so that he faced her. He could see the sweat on her forehead, on her upper lip and dripping down her throat to disappear under the open neck of her safari shirt. For one wild moment he wanted to brush it away. Lick it away. He wanted to touch her, but he forced that out of his mind.

"I'm not endangering anyone," he said. "I'm here to help."

"By taking the men out to die in some kind of heroic fight. A fight they can't win."

"If we don't do this, the enemy will be here before we have a chance to do anything about it. There will be a wholesale slaughter."

"But if you hadn't come," she snapped, "then the . . ."

"Makes no difference now," interrupted Bromhead. "We can't take back the fact that we're here. If I had known a few more things about this village, then I might not have come. But I didn't know them and I did come. I have to live with that. And I have to live with my obligation to these people."

"I hope the villagers can live with it, too."

"That's why we're going out. To make sure they can. Maybe the only thing we'll do is hold up the Communists for a couple of days. If that's the case, then the people have a chance to slip

away. Now get out of here and let me get to work." Bromhead
stood, took a step toward her and then stopped.

"Why don't you get out?" she asked. "Just leave. Then the
Communists have no reason to come here."

"Doesn't work that way. The Communists will wipe out this
village to prove a point. They will kill everyone here as an example."

"You can't know that," she said.

"But I can. They've done it before. The Soviets did it. Sta-
lin wiped out a whole class of people because they wouldn't
give up their small farms. Six million people dead and no world
cry against it. The red Chinese did it during the revolutions.
More thousands dead. When the Communists take over, they
always kill thousands. They've done it time and again. What's
to stop them from eliminating a small village in the mountains in Laos?"

"Then you knew what would happen when you came," she
accused. "You knew what they would do and you still came.
Even knowing that, you came." She was on her feet, her face
a mask of outrage.

"I know what they'll do if South Vietnam falls. This village
and a hundred like it will cease to exist. The Communists will
sweep through here and round up the people, moving them to
relocation camps and in those camps millions will die. By
coming here, I provide these people with the weapons and the
ability to fight for their lives. I've brought none of this down
on these people." His voice was rising as he spoke, the anger
flowing through him like an increasing electrical current. "I
may have speeded up the process, but that's all I've done. I
didn't make the situation."

"You're an arrogant, obnoxious pawn who doesn't know
shit!" she screamed.

Bromhead smiled at that, wondering how he could think of
her as attractive. Her whole attitude had been formed in a

dreamworld, one that didn't exist, although it was impossible to convince her of that. She thought all people were honorable and it would be a long time before she realized they weren't. A long time before she realized that most people were motivated by self-interest. He said, "Your kind always turn to personal insults when you have no argument."

"My kind?" she said.

"You pinko university liberals."

Now she smiled. "You got them all there. Everyone of the clichés used by the military. Pinko university liberals."

"Then why aren't the university types in the streets over the North Vietnamese atrocities? The North Vietnamese propose holiday cease-fires and then break them at will. The Communists, the North Vietnamese violate the neutrality of Laos and Cambodia and no one cares. Every Communist country sends supplies to the North Vietnamese and no one cares. Hell, there are even advisers from Red China in South Vietnam and no one cares."

"That's different," said Lucas.

"How? How in the hell is it different? We're talking about one thing here."

"The North Vietnamese asked for the help."

"Well, so the fuck did the South Vietnamese and so would these people here, if they had a way to do it. You saw how we were treated when we arrived. Like honored guests, not as invaders. They can't wait to get out and kill the Communists."

"That's only because you brought new weapons. Gifts for them."

"Well, I don't see any Vietnamese or the Pathet Lao arriving with gifts of any kind. And I hear a lot of talk about killing the Communists."

"I knew it would do no good coming here," she said. "I thought that I could reason with you, that you had some intelligence, but I see that I was wrong. I just hope you don't get too many of these people killed.'' With that she moved rapidly to the door.

As she ducked out, Bromhead called after her, ''I hope *you* don't get them all killed.''

7

THE MEO VILLAGE, LAOS

Long before dawn the men assembled near one of the corner bunkers. Work on them had been continued the day before, although most of Bromhead's and Gilman's time had been spent getting the ambush patrol ready. Those villagers not involved with it had been assigned to the bunker detail, and although the progress had been slow, two of the bunkers had been finished and eight more had been started.

At two in the morning, the last of the scouts returned. He went directly to Beu's hootch, who escorted him to the weapons hut where Bromhead slept. The man was filthy, covered with dirt, sweat and a hundred scratches. He had lost his crossbow but he had found the enemy. A column of soldiers moving to the south following a small, ill-defined trail. When questioned about the number he would only say, "Many. Many," and then *"beaucoup,"* one of the few French words he knew.

Bromhead finally sent the man away and used a map to determine how far the enemy was and his route of travel. Showing the scout a map did no good because the man couldn't read it. The symbols were so much nonsense to him. Gilman and

Bromhead plotted a course, figuring where the enemy column would be the next day.

Afterward, they went through the equipment one last time. They unpacked several claymore mines, hand grenades, and anything else they thought might be useful in the ambush. Bromhead wanted to do more, but while standing in the litter of equipment he could think of nothing else. At best, they would be gone the majority of one day and at worst, two. A few cans of C-rations, an extra canteen or two, and that was it.

Bromhead finally settled down to rest. He slept fitfully, waking up with a start every few minutes. He would jerk awake, his nerves screaming, his senses alert, as if he had heard something outside. Finally he got up, moved to the outside of the hootch where he could sit on the edge of the floor in the doorway and watch the world.

The moon was up, giving the surroundings the strange, black and white look of an old movie. There was a light ground fog that hugged the low spots and almost no breeze. Bromhead pulled at some of the thatch and wrapped it around his finger, watching the jungle. It was a black, ominous place beyond the grassy plain. A foreboding· place that seemed to beckon him. He felt chills up and down his spine as if he were looking at the moors in England where the phantom had just vanished. All he needed was the howling of a wolf in the background and it would be the perfect setting for a horror story.

But he didn't move. He turned so that he was looking at the village. The rows of hootches, each up on stilts, the bare ground under it visible. There was a flickering of firelight and he saw a dog trotting along. Nothing else was moving. Nothing else was making any noise. It was as quiet as death and that made the setting even more ominous.

Behind him, he heard a scrape of leather on wood and looked over his shoulder.

"You worried, Colonel?" asked Gilman.

Bromhead took a breath and sighed. "Worried? What the hell is there to be worried about? We're going to chase down a large NVA column, with a bunch of men who were trained by someone else using weapons that belong in the Second World War. Why worry?"

"Sure, Colonel. Why worry?"

"Listen, tomorrow, keep an eye on Hansen. He's not that experienced, either."

"Yes, sir."

"And Nick, you watch out for yourself, too."

"Sure. I always do." He hesitated and then said, "Guess I'll go take a piss."

Bromhead stood and ducked into the hootch. He wiped a hand over his face, felt the stubble, the sweat, and rubbed it on his shirt. "Think I'll catch a little sleep. Be about an hour or so."

He hadn't slept during that hour. He had thought about the mission and that scared him. He forced those thoughts from his mind and planned a model railroad for when he returned to the World. An HO railroad with lots of boxcars and a steam engine. That did it and before he knew it, Gilman was moving around. Hansen sat up, checked the time and began to collect his equipment.

As the three of them left the weapons hootch, they saw that Beu had collected his men and had them ready. Bromhead and Gilman checked the weapons while Hansen inspected the rest. He scrutinized their pistol belts, canteens and first-aid kits.

Standing there in the early morning mist, the sunlight just beginning to drive the night away, Bromhead briefed the men in French while Beu translated. They had to maintain unit integrity, maintain interval and be patient. If they did those things, they would not be hurt and they would kill a lot of the Communists. That was met with a rousing cheer. Bromhead started, but said nothing. With luck, there were no enemy soldiers around to hear the men cheering, and if there were, then it was too late to do anything about it.

And it was then that Gilman pulled Bromhead to the side. "Sir, I've got a problem."

Bromhead shot a glance at the Meos and at Beu, then leaned close to Gilman. "What is it?"

"Think I picked up a dose."

"A dose?" asked Bromhead.

"Yes, sir. The clap. I think I caught a dose of it."

Bromhead shook his head. "One hell of a time to tell me."

"I thought maybe you could get me some pills or something. I heard that you Special Forces guys take penicillin and that takes care of it. Just get me some pills and I'll be fine."

"Damn it all to hell," muttered Bromhead. "If this isn't always the way. I knew coming out without the medic was going to fucking kill us. Christ, I don't know if penicillin pills will cure it. Shit. About the only thing I know is that it has to be treated."

"But not now, sir," said Gilman.

Bromhead rubbed a hand over his head. "Well that does explain a couple of things. You know, I really should leave you here. We can't have you dropping out of the formation every hour to piss."

"Get me the pills and I'll be fine."

Bromhead stared at him for a long time. He was a dark gray shape outlined by the faint glow of a fire. "Damn it all anyway."

"The pills, sir," said Gilman.

"Major Hansen, you take charge here for a few minutes while Major Gilman and I converse on an urgent matter."

Hansen didn't look pleased, but he said nothing.

At the hootch, Bromhead went through the medical kit, found a bottle of pills and checked them. As he dumped several into his hand, he said, "I don't know anything about this. Are you allergic to penicillin?"

"Not that I know of," said Gilman.

"Well, here, take four now and another four in a couple of hours. You have a discharge or anything? You dripping?"

"A little. Not much."

"At least you had the good sense to head into the jungle to piss so that you don't infect the village."

"Yes, sir."

Bromhead shook his head again. "This is exactly what we needed. I knew we'd need a medic before this was over. Hell, we haven't taken a casualty yet and we need the medic." He watched as Gilman swallowed the tablets, washing them down with water from his canteen. When he was finished, Bromhead said, "Let's go find the patrol and get going."

As the sun peeked over the horizon, the patrol moved out, a long column of men with Bromhead, Hansen and Beu in the lead and Gilman bringing up the rear where he could discreetly take care of his problem. They crossed the open, grassy plain quickly and entered the jungle. Travel at first was slow because it was still dark on the ground, but as the sun rose, the shadows lightened and the earth took on the twilight of a dense jungle so that they could move faster. They spread out more, using a trail that led lower into a wide valley with a small stream bubbling through its center. They crossed it quickly and turned to the north.

The jungle around them opened up slightly, the dense vegetation giving way to lighter scrub at the base of the giant trees. Bromhead and Beu used their machetes to hack at the vines and branches. At first the work was easy, the machete seeming to cut through the plants on its own, but the heat and humidity sapped Bromhead's strength until it felt as if the machete weighed twenty pounds. Finally he let one of the others take the point, Bromhead walking right behind him, a compass in one hand and his map in the other.

By midmorning they came to a wide trail. It was a well used path that had sandal prints in the soft dirt where it was visible. Most of it was carpeted by decaying vegetation.

Bromhead halted the column and stood watching as they slipped deeper into the jungle. He and Gilman then went on ahead, looking for a good ambush spot. They wanted a straight section of the trail so that they could see the whole column at once. They wanted a place that would offer them protection and have a limited amount for the enemy. That was the ideal. Bromhead figured they would have to settle for something less.

They found the spot not more than half a klick away. There was a rocky outcropping along the eastern side of the trail that was the perfect place for Bromhead's patrol. On the other side was a slight depression that would offer the enemy sanctuary from the fire pouring into them. That was even better. If . Bromhead planted his claymores in that ditch, he could trigger them as the enemy retreated there. It would be a devastating blow to them, creating panic.

They hurried back to the main body of the patrol, got them on their feet and moved them into position. Bromhead, Gilman and Beu set the men, telling them that they were responsible for the section of the trail immediately in front of them. They were to shoot when they had a target and stop when they didn't. The signal to fire would be an explosion. Bromhead planned to toss grenades and had told both Gilman and Hansen to do the same with him.

When the men were ready, Bromhead and Hansen worked their way to the trail, stood there for a moment and then crossed it. Bromhead placed one of the claymore mines so that it would fire down the ditch. He anchored it against a tree, and played out the firing cables, covering them with dirt and vegetation. Hansen put another at the far end, firing back toward the first. Together, they planted three others that were set at angles so they would rake the likely hiding places. After they covered the cables, they crossed the path and found firing positions among the rocks. Bromhead laid the firing controls out in front of him so that he would know which mine would fire.

The ambush itself was laid out parallel to the trail. There were three men about a hundred meters behind them to prevent a counterattack from the rear. Bromhead sent another man half a klick to the north to watch for the enemy, with instructions to come back when he saw the head of the column. And there were two men to the south of Bromhead's patrol to make sure that they didn't get caught by an unexpected move by the enemy.

Then there was nothing left to do but wait. Sit in the jungle, listening to the noises around him, the animals moving through the trees or along the ground. There was a quiet rustling near him and Bromhead watched a snake appear, moving toward a patch of sunlight on a section of rock. It stopped there, ignoring everything around it, basking in the sun. Bromhead studied it, trying to identify it, wondering if it was poisonous. All he knew was that the majority of the snakes in Southeast Asia were poisonous and some of the poisons were extremely deadly. He decided that the first thing he would do, after tossing his grenades, was shoot the snake.

He suddenly felt thirsty. Since the scout had not reappeared, Bromhead slowly took out his canteen, his eyes on the snake only twelve feet away, and unscrewed the cap. He tilted it to his mouth and drank deeply. The water was warm and tasted of plastic. He let some of it drip down his chin and neck. That cooled him momentarily. He put the canteen down where he could get it again without having to unsnap a cover.

Then he sat still, watching the snake and listening to the jungle. He flexed his muscles so that they didn't stiffen or cramp. He had to keep the blood circulating. He concentrated on his breathing, keeping it regular. It was something to do while he waited.

THE AIR FORCE C-123 left Tan Son Nhut, climbed high into the bright blue morning sky, and turned to the north once it reached altitude. Gerber sat in the red webbing of the troop seat, his rucksack at his feet and tied down by a long cable that had been applied by the loadmaster just prior to takeoff. He held his M-16 in both hands, the butt on the deck, the barrel pointing toward the top of the fuselage. He had stripped the magazine from it and ejected the chambered round.

Fetterman sat beside him, his head back and eyes closed. While the plane sat on the ground, he had been sweating, but once airborne, he had cooled off, still not opening his eyes.

They landed briefly at Ban Me Thuot, Pleiku, and Kontum, to let off passengers, discharge cargo, and then pick up passengers and new cargo. At Kontum, Gerber and Fetterman exited into the stifling midmorning heat. The loadmaster tossed their equipment out the door to land in the soft red dirt at the edge of the taxiway.

They picked it up, and walked across the blazing PSP to the tiny terminal building. To one side, two Huey helicopters sat unattended, their blades tied down. Gerber dropped his equipment to the ground and told Fetterman to watch it.

Inside he found a typical terminal. A few broken-down chairs for those awaiting rides, a long, low counter, and behind that a scheduling board. A short, thin man with badly peeling skin and thin blond hair was using a black grease pencil to make a note on the scheduling board. He wore a sweat-damp, OD green T-shirt, jungle fatigue pants and jungle boots.

When he dropped to the floor and turned around, Gerber asked, "You got anything going north to any of the Special Forces camps?"

The man leaned on the counter. "Which one?"

"Preferably A-245 at Dak Seang, but anything up in that area will do. Dak To or Dak Sut."

"You want a chopper or what?"

"Anything."

The man pulled a loose-leaf notebook across the counter and flipped it open. He leafed through the pages until he found what he wanted. "Think we've space on a chopper out about two this afternoon. That'll give you time for some lunch and to see all our sights. Name?"

"There's two of us and some equipment."

"Shouldn't be a problem. Name?"

Gerber gave it to him, and a list of the equipment that they carried. Before he left, the man said, "Remember, this ain't no scheduled airline. It's best you be here 'bout an hour earlier. That way, if the flight crew gets antsy, you'll be here to fly out 'cause they ain't gonna wait."

"Thanks," said Gerber.

THE WAIT TURNED OUT TO BE relatively short. An hour after the scout was sent, he returned. He whispered to Beu, who then moved down to Bromhead. "Communists come now. Many of them. Tau saw only a few but heard many more. They are on the trail." He grinned, showing broken, yellowed teeth that had been filed to points.

"All right," said Bromhead. "It is imperative that no one moves now. We don't want to tip our hand. Everyone must wait for the explosions before they shoot. If they don't we won't be able to kill all the Communists."

"The men understand," said Beu.

"Then get ready," said Bromhead.

Beu moved to the right several feet and crouched among the rocks. He held his carbine in both hands, waiting.

Bromhead looked at the rock, but the snake had slithered away. He hoped that it was wending its way to the trail, not coming closer to him. He felt the hair on the back of his neck stand on end and there was a tingling at the base of his spine. It wasn't the coming action that caused it, but the disappearance of the snake. That scared him more than the approaching enemy because he knew it was out there, but not where it was.

He kept his eyes moving, searching the ground, but the snake was gone. He felt his ears twitch at the slightest sound, but when he turned to look, the source of the noise was gone. His attention was wandering, distracted by the snake, but he couldn't help it. It was out there, waiting for the opportunity to strike. The only thing he knew about it was that it wasn't a cobra. He was sure that he would recognize a cobra.

And then he heard the enemy column. They had no noise discipline. The men were talking, their equipment rattling. It meant that they were at home in this section of the jungle and that they feared nothing in it. They were out for a stroll, and they would destroy the first village they found. That was assuming that these men had been sent to destroy the village. Bromhead didn't care why they were there.

The point, four men grouped together, appeared in the distance. All wore the OD green of the NVA, which didn't surprise Bromhead. They wore pistol belts holding their canteens, chest pouches for the banana clips for their weapons, pith helmets with red stars on them, and carried AK-47s. Two of them had slung their weapons, one carried his in his hands, and one had leaned the rifle on his shoulder, clutching the barrel.

The point passed Bromhead, the men looking neither right nor left. It was as if they didn't have a care in the world. Ten or twelve feet behind them was the leader of the column.

Bromhead prayed that the men of his patrol would have the patience to wait. If the ambush was sprung too early, the

Communists would get away. They would be able to escape the way they came, running quickly out of small arms range and out of sight.

The head of the column reached Bromhead and behind them he could see a hundred men, maybe more. Now he wondered if the ambush would be large enough to contain the whole column. He reached down and picked up one of his grenades. Slowly, his eyes fixed on the enemy soldiers, he pulled the pin. He held the spoon tightly.

The point reached the far side of the ambush as the end of the column approached. There was nothing he could do to keep the point inside the killing zone. He had to let the point go. Four men couldn't cause that much trouble if the rest of the column was shot to pieces.

When he saw the rear, Bromhead turned and threw his grenade at it. In the same motion he snagged a second grenade, jerked the pin free and tossed it at the trail. Then he dropped flat and grabbed at his M-1 carbine.

A second later there was an explosion. It was followed by a second and a few moments after that, three more. Bromhead lifted his head and saw the column disintegrate. The enemy soldiers were shouting, screaming, crying. Rifle fire broke out, raking the trail with a deadly accuracy. Bromhead could see the bullets hitting the ground, kicking up the dirt and striking the men still there. He saw bodies falling and ripped apart. There were splashes of blood, the bright red staining the dark browns and deep greens of the jungle.

The firing increased as all the men with Bromhead opened fire, pulling the triggers as fast as they could. The enemy, shocked, momentarily standing there, confused, turned to flee.

Bromhead saw the North Vietnamese soldiers falling and dying. They were missing hands or arms or heads. Bodies tumbled on top of one another. Bodies dropping all around as the sound of the shooting increased until it was a roar that eclipsed all others in the jungle.

Some of the Vietnamese dived to the ditch and turned. They poked the barrels of their AKs into the open and began to shoot. First only a couple of them, and then more of them as those still alive vacated the trail, leaving the dead behind.

As the enemy bullets began to snap the air around him, Bromhead dropped his carbine and seized the firing controls of the claymores. He stuck his head up, glanced at the enemy soldiers and let two of the controls fall to the rock. He held the one, peeked again and then fired.

From behind the trail came the explosion. Hundreds of tiny steel balls cut through the air, slamming into the rear of the enemy. There were shouts of surprise. Screams of pain. Shrieks of panic. Men died as blood blossomed out their chests or stomachs or fountained from their throats. They collapsed in heaps.

Again Bromhead looked up. The NVA were still holding the ditch, putting out rounds. He dropped down, hugging the sun-hot rock. He scooped the remaining claymore controls and punched them all off. There was a series of explosions that blew the resistance out of the enemy. Firing from the ditch tapered off until it was sporadic. Bromhead grabbed his rifle and sighted. He could see two men moving, one of them running hunched over, zigzagging in and out of the trees and bushes.

Bromhead aimed at the other man. He squeezed the trigger, felt the weapon fire. The enemy soldier jerked once and reached behind him as if to brush an insect from his shoulder. He stumbled and fell, losing his weapon. But then he was up again, running, disappearing into the trees.

Bromhead turned and looked down on the ambush. His men were up, some of them out from their cover, firing into the bodies lying on the trail. There was no return fire. Bromhead looked at Beu who was still shooting, burning through his ammo as fast as he could fire.

"That's it!" yelled Bromhead. "Cease fire! Cease fire! *Cessez tirant!*"

Beu looked up, startled. He lowered his weapon and grinned as he saw the bodies scattered on the trail and among the bushes and ferns around it. Then he began to shout for his men to stop shooting. The cry was taken up by others until the shooting died away.

For a few minutes Bromhead stayed where he was, watching the trail. He saw no movement along it or behind it. There was no evidence that any of the enemy still lived. He got slowly to his feet and climbed out of hiding. He moved carefully, watching for some kind of trick.

This was the thing that he hated the most. Checking the bodies. Not because he was repulsed by the dead, but because it was so damned dangerous. Many good men had been killed or wounded by dying soldiers who figured they might as well take one more with them.

Once on the trail, it was obvious to him that most of the enemy were dead. Their bodies had been badly broken in the firing. Arms and legs ripped off, stomachs laid open so that the entrails spilled out. Heads with holes so big that the brains had slid out. There was blood everywhere and already the flies were beginning to land, creating black spots in the pools. The trail was a mess, looking and smelling worse than a slaughterhouse. Within moments, flies had begun to swarm, filling the silence with their buzzing.

Gilman approached, his carbine clutched in his hands. The barrel was pointed at the enemy bodies as if he expected them to react to him.

"We've four dead and seven wounded," he said.

"How bad are the wounded?"

"Two aren't in very good shape. One man was grazed in the head by a round and the other four are crippled right now, but should be okay. Hansen's treating them."

"Some got away," said Bromhead.

"Yes, sir. Want me to organize a party to look for them?" asked Gilman.

Bromhead knew what Fetterman would do. He would take off and track down each of the enemy soldiers who had escaped, but Fetterman was exceptional. There was no one else like him in South Vietnam. Besides, Bromhead didn't think the enemy soldiers would pose that much of a threat. When they stopped running, they would find themselves lost in some of the worst jungle in the world. If they survived that, it would take them a long time, several days, to find help.

"No," he told Gilman. "You'd never get them all. I saw one man run back the way they came, one run into the jungle opposite us, and the point had to break the other way. They're scattered all over the place."

"So what do we do now?"

"Collect the weapons, or rather as many as we can carry. Destroy the others and then get the fuck out of here."

"Yes, sir." Gilman turned and shouted at several of the men. They began picking up the dropped AKs and SKSs, stacking them away from the trail.

As they worked, Bromhead said, "You see a snake around here anywhere?"

"Seen a couple of them," said Gilman. "You looking for a specific one?"

Bromhead had to laugh. "No. I saw one just before we sprung the ambush and I was afraid of stepping on it. I'd just like to know what happened to it."

"I'll keep an eye open and if I see it, I'll give you a shout."

Bromhead pointed at Beu. "Colonel, recall the men from the rear of the ambush and prepare to move out. We don't want to remain here too long."

"They come when they heard the shooting. They didn't want to miss anything."

"Great," he said sarcastically. "You get some people to the rear now and have them watch. Get a couple of men a hundred meters up and down the trail. I want to get out of here in a couple of minutes."

Beu nodded.

"Colonel," said Bromhead, "I want you to understand that we can't have men leaving their positions. They could jeopardize the whole patrol. If the enemy had mounted a counter-attack we would have had no warning."

"I understand."

"You get those men out there and tell them not to move until they get instructions."

With that, Beu took off to organize the security. Bromhead wandered around the ambush site, checking on everything. The men were picking up the weapons and stacking them at the side of the trail. Others were building stretchers for the wounded and the dead. They were using their poncho liners and long, flexible saplings cut from the jungle. By laying the liners over the poles and using the weight of the body to hold it in place, they had an effective stretcher.

Normally he would have buried the dead where they fell, but Bromhead didn't want the enemy to find them and identify the attackers. Besides, the Meos wouldn't leave their dead because they believed that an unburied body was cursed to roam the Earth looking for its grave, and that grave had to be in a certain place.

Within thirty minutes they were ready to move out. Each of the men had two captured weapons, the ammo for them, and his own weapon. The rest of the SKSs were stacked and

Bromhead was prepared to blow them up with a couple of hand grenades as soon as everyone was clear.

Before they moved out, Bromhead pulled Beu to the side. "We don't take the easy trail back. We could use it coming down because no one was looking for us, but now they know we're here and to use it again is suicide."

"I understand."

"Good. Then move them out. Major Gilman and I will catch up in a few minutes."

Hansen approached and said, "Stretchers are ready and so are the wounded."

"Keep them in the middle of the column. If there is a problem, don't be afraid to call a halt, but don't take too long."

"Yes, sir." Hansen returned to the main column to give the orders.

"Okay, Colonel Beu," said Bromhead. "Let's get going."

Beu nodded, trotted to the front of the column. He halted there, looked over his shoulder and waved a hand. "Forward," he commanded.

As they moved out, Bromhead asked, "What's the best way to do this?"

"Stack up everything, ammo, grenades, everything, and toss a willie pete into the middle of it. The detonation should damage everything and destroy most of it. The fire will take care of the rest."

"Then let's do it."

They moved down the trail and Bromhead handed Gilman a white phosphorus grenade. "On three?"

"Sure."

Bromhead pulled the pin, counted to three and both men tossed the grenades at the same time. They turned and ran, and three seconds later there were twin explosions behind them. They could hear some of the rounds cooking off, popping and whizzing as the burning white phosphorus spread.

"If there was anything of use left, they'll be hard pressed to find it."

"Yes, sir," said Gilman.

They took off then, hurrying to catch up with the patrol. When they spotted it twenty minutes later, they slowed to a walk. "That was a good ambush," said Gilman. "Well planned and very well done."

"You saying that because you don't think an army officer knows what he's doing?"

"No, sir. Said it because we didn't know how these guys would do. They did very well for a bunch of amateurs and didn't make many mistakes."

"That's right," said Bromhead. "I was surprised that we could convince them to let the enemy walk right by without shooting at them, but they sat there quietly until we triggered the ambush."

"Sign of good training."

"Yeah," said Bromhead. "Now let's just get the hell out of here."

8

THE JUNGLES OF LAOS
NEAR THE HO CHI MINH
TRAIL

An hour after the ambush and two klicks away from it, Beu halted the column. They spread out in a loose circle, half the men eating the food they had carried, the other half watching the jungle, waiting for the enemy to return. Bromhead moved around the circle, checking on the men, their weapons and their equipment. He noticed that the heat and humidity were beginning to take their toll on the Meos. They didn't seem to like being in the valley where the humidity hung thick like yesterday's underwear, and they didn't like being away from the mountain where the village was located.

He said nothing to them, just noticed the first signs of fatigue. They were being a little careless with their weapons and were complaining about taking the long way home. He had heard Beu tell several of them that the direct route was now the most dangerous. Still, it didn't make them happy.

After an hour's break, the men rested and weapons checked, they began the march home. There were now three point men, each armed with a machete so that they could chop their way through the vegetation.

They kept at it, the sweat pouring from them, soaking their uniforms, until one of the men could stand it no more. He buried the blade of his machete in the trunk of a tree and stripped off his shirt. He wadded it into a ball and tossed it away. As it disappeared in the jungle, he jerked his machete free so that he could continue to work.

Because of the heat, they halted again to rest and to drink water. Bromhead drained one of his canteens, pouring some of it over his head in an attempt to cool off. He wiped the water from his face and rubbed it on the back of his neck. It didn't refresh him completely, but it helped.

Once more they started struggling up the rocky side of the mountain. Progress slowed to a crawl as the afternoon slipped away and the light began to fade. Bromhead had been concerned that they would not make it back to the village before dark, but tactics dictated the plan. Never use the same trail twice.

When they halted for another rest break, Bromhead searched out Hansen to find out if any of the wounded were in immediate danger.

Hansen was sitting with his back to a tree, his legs straight out in front of him. His face was pale and he was covered with sweat. He had removed his helmet and his hair hung in dark strands around his face.

"Christ man, are you all right?" asked Bromhead.

"Tired. Didn't know walking through the jungle was so hard."

"We're not walking, we're humping. There's a difference and I think that you've just learned it."

"I think so, too."

"You drink any water?"

"As much as I could stand."

"Well, you'll have plenty of time to rest. I think we'll camp here for the night. Put out a couple of short patrols to make sure we're not being followed. Everyone else gets a good night's sleep."

"I can use it."

"Yeah," agreed Bromhead. He sat down beside Hansen and took off his helmet. "How're the wounded doing? Anyone in danger of dying if we don't press on?"

"Haven't checked them in a couple of hours. Last time I looked, they were resting comfortably. Bleeding had stopped."

"You haven't checked on them for a couple of hours?" asked Bromhead.

"Well, an hour or so maybe. Told the stretcher bearers to let me know if anyone suddenly took a turn for the worse. And then I was busy just trying to keep up with the column."

"I understand," said Bromhead. "Why don't you take a look now and let me know how they are?"

With an effort, Hansen picked up his helmet and got to his feet. He stood there for a moment, looking as if he was about to faint. Then he shook his head and moved off.

Bromhead went in search of Gilman. The Marine was sitting on the ground, his back to a teak tree, eating from a can of beans and franks. He grinned at Bromhead. "These are better heated, but we can't risk a fire."

"How come you always get the good stuff?" asked Bromhead.

"Because I go through the boxes and pick it out. Who wants to lug a can of ham and lima beans through the jungle when there is actually some good stuff in there?"

"Good point. How are you doing?"

"Pills helped a little, but not enough." Gilman looked down at his crotch. "Burns to piss and it's dripping now."

"Without a shot, I don't think I can help you. They use the penicillin pills after the massive injections. I'm afraid we're only making things worse this way."

"Christ, sir, I'm sorry about this." He face changed to a mask and he stuffed the spoon into the can. "What're we going to do?"

"If we can get a medic in, we'll be in good shape. Otherwise you're going to have to be evacced and that's going to piss off the people in Saigon."

"Because I got a dose?"

"No." Bromhead shook his head. "Because you were dumb enough to do it on the way to a covert mission."

Hansen appeared then, looking even paler. "They're gone," he said in a tremulous voice. "The wounded are gone and no one will tell me where. You don't think they shot them do you?"

That was exactly what Bromhead thought and then he remembered their belief that the dead needed a grave. A marked grave. "No," he said. "Come on Nick, let's find Beu and ask him."

THE CHOPPER RIDE FROM PLEIKU to the Special Forces camp at Dak To was a wild one. The pilot never got more than three feet above the trees as he slipped through the mountain valleys and over the tops of the hills that looked like a huge green sea spread out in front of him. They were jerked up and down, at first seeming to float against the seat belts and then forced toward the deck by a giant, unseen hand. With the roar of the wind through the open cargo compartment doors, the scream of the turbine engine, and the snapping and popping of the rotor system, there was no way to be heard.

Gerber sat in the center of the troop seat, his back to the transmission, at first watching the jungle through the windshield and then turning so that he could see out the cargo compartment door. As far as he could see there was a vast sea of unbroken green. It swelled and dipped, the motion of the helicopter giving the jungle the appearance of ocean waves.

He shot a glance at Fetterman, who was watching it all with a grin on his face. Gerber knew that Fetterman was thinking there were people in the World who paid good money for just such a ride. They would wait in long lines to be thrilled by the latest marvel in roller coasters or water slides. Fetterman was getting it all for free, or even better, was being paid to do it.

In the distance Gerber saw a break in the green. A cloud of dark smoke seemed to point at the circle of a Special Forces camp at the top of a hill. The helicopter begin a climb, the nose pointed at the camp.

Seconds later they were over it and the chopper rolled up on its side so that the camp was visible straight down, out the left door. They dropped from the sky, seemingly out of control as the pilot held a tight circle over the camp. At the last second, he rolled out straight, hauled back on the cyclic so that the aircraft was nearly standing on its tail, all the aerodynamic capabilities of the chopper destroyed. Then as the nose fell and the skids leveled, the pilot pulled in an armload of pitch and the helicopter eased to the ground, the skids touching it lightly.

Gerber unfastened his seat belt, and started to stand, but his knees were weak. He grabbed his equipment, slapped the pilot on the back of the head to get his attention, then held up a thumb.

He jumped to the ground, waited until Fetterman climbed out, then moved back. The chopper picked up to a hover, the rotor wash snagging the debris scattered around and swirling it into a whirlwind of dust and dirt. A second later the aircraft turned, the nose dumped and it began racing along the runway, gaining speed. As it neared the end of the runway, where the jungle had tried to recapture some of the cleared land, it leaped skyward, climbing out rapidly.

When the helicopter was gone, a man left the protection of the camp, walked along the road that led to the runway and stopped at the edge. "You Gerber and Fetterman?"

Gerber nodded. "I'm Gerber and he's Fetterman."

"Yes, sir. I'm Sergeant Davies. Captain asked me to escort you inside and see what all you need."

Gerber shouldered his gear. "Lead on."

Inside the camp, a small Special Forces base like so many others, Gerber and Fetterman were taken to the team house. On the way, Gerber saw the sandbagged structures that had to be the commo bunker, the command post at the base of the observation tower, and the dispensary, nearly buried underground with only the roof showing. They were taken down a short flight into the dim recesses of the team house.

It looked like almost every other team house that Gerber had ever been in. There were tables surrounded by chairs. At the far end was a bar and behind it, a woman stood, cutting vegetables with a giant knife.

Davies pointed at the man sitting by himself. "That's our CO." He approached and added, "Captain Blanchfeld, this is Captain Gerber and Sergeant Fetterman."

Blanchfeld got up and shook hands with both men. The captain was a tall, stocky man who looked as if he had lost a number of fistfights, some of them recently. There were scars on his right cheek and forehead. His nose had been broken and there was a scab on his chin. He had thick eyebrows and thinning hair. He waved at a couple of unoccupied chairs. "Have a seat. You want some grub?"

"That would be fine," said Gerber.

The captain turned to Davies. "Have Lei bring our guests some food and find them a couple of beers." He turned back to Gerber and Fetterman. "Water's really foul and the milk is spoiled and some of the men would kill just to see a Coke can, let alone for what might be in it."

Gerber thought of the rows of cans that Maxwell had on his desk and how easy it was to find Coke in Saigon and Bien Hoa. And he thought about all the men who talked about how rough they had it, being away from home and their families as they chased the local women, dined on steak and told each other that war was hell.

A young woman, her face badly scared by fire, brought the food and set plates in front of Gerber and Fetterman. She grinned shyly at both of them and then fled. Davies arrived with the beer.

"I'm afraid it's warm, but what the hell?"

"That's all right," said Fetterman. "At least it's wet and that's what counts."

As they started to eat, Blanchfeld asked, "Radio message was a bit cryptic. Just what do you need?"

Gerber put his fork down. "We'd like to arrange to have a company of strikers on standby in case we need to make an insertion into Laos."

"Uh-huh," said Blanchfeld. "And given the way you've slipped in here, I suppose you have all the paperwork on it."

"Of course," said Gerber, grinning. Both officers knew that no paperwork would ever exist on the mission, if there was one. "The deal is, I've got my old exec on a covert just on the other side of the border and his butt is hanging out. I'd like to be in a position to make sure that Charlie doesn't kick it up between his shoulder blades."

"What do you want me to do?" asked Blanchfeld.

"Just give us a strike company if we need it, and the use of a radio so that we can coordinate airlift if we have to. I don't think there's going to be a problem, but if there is, I want to be around to help."

Blanchfeld dug a pack of cigarettes out of his pocket and shook one out. He lit it, breathed deeply and exhaled a cloud of blue. "I think the first-strike company would be the best. I'll have them standing by."

"Might come to nothing," said Gerber. "If nothing happens in the next week or so, we'll just fade away."

"In the meantime," said Blanchfeld, "I'll put you to work."

BEU WAS WITH A GROUP of his men, each holding an AK-47 as if it was a trophy. He smiled at the Americans as they approached. "We have done well."

"So far," said Bromhead. "Now, tell me where the wounded are. What have you done with them?"

"Wounded have been taken care of."

Hansen was looking from one man to the other, trying to understand what was being said. He stared at Gilman and demanded, "What's happening?"

"Nothing yet," hissed Gilman.

"What do you mean they've been taken care of?" said Bromhead. "You didn't kill them, did you?"

"No, of course not. Wounded on the way home. On the way to the village."

Bromhead felt the blood drain from his face. His stomach knotted up as he realized what it meant. "How are they on the way home?"

"Too hard carrying stretchers this way. Ground too rough. I tell the men to take the trail home." He grinned, still not understanding what was taking place. "They should be to the village now. In time for evening meal."

Bromhead spoke slowly, as if lecturing a child. "I want you to listen carefully. You may have blown us out of the water. If the NVA or VC pick up the trail, your men are going to lead them to your village. Right to them."

Understanding dawned on Beu's face. He stood up but didn't speak.

"We have got to get going. Now!" said Bromhead. "We do not have time to rest, time to sleep, time to eat or do anything. We must hurry."

Beu nodded and moved around the perimeter alerting his troops. Bromhead pulled out his map, folded it and crouched.

He laid it against his knee and pointed. "We should be about here. The trail they used is here, maybe three, four klicks away. If we cut through the jungle here, we can reach it and follow it back to the village."

"That a good idea, Colonel?" asked Gilman.

"No, it's a terrible one. But, if the NVA or VC are following the wounded, we might come up behind them. Give them a surprise."

"Or we could walk into an ambush ourselves, effectively cutting off aid," said Gilman.

"I think that's a chance we're going to have to take. We have got to make some time and by following our current route, we won't reach the village before tomorrow morning."

"I understand, Colonel," said Gilman. "I would like to hang back a klick or so with five or ten men as a rear guard. I can bail you out."

"How are you feeling now?"

"If I was dying, I wouldn't tell you," said Gilman, a smile on his face.

"Good," said Bromhead. "Very good, but you can only have five. We'll load you down with grenades."

IT WAS LATE AFTERNOON when Jane Lucas decided that she had to do something. She had spent most of the day wandering around the village, passing the weapons hootch frequently. Although no one had bothered to consult her, she knew what was happening. Too many of the men were gone, as were the three Americans. They were out, taking the war to the suspected enemy.

And since all three of them had gone, it meant that the weapons hut was unguarded. Finally she stopped in front of the door and looked up into the dim interior. She stepped up on the notched log and peered inside. She could see the outlines of the boxes and crates and equipment. Guiltily she looked over her shoulder and then scurried up the notched log and into the hootch.

She dropped to her knees in front of a crate marked Ammunition, Ball, .30 Caliber. Ignoring everything, she levered her fingers under the wooden cover and tried to pull it free. When that didn't work, she found a scrap of wood and used it as a crowbar. The top came off with a screech of protesting nails. Inside was just what the crate had said: Ammunition, Ball, .30 Caliber.

She glanced to the right and saw cardboard boxes that contained C-ration meals. Others holding grenades, or flares, or weapons. Everything that the modern army needed to kill human beings, she thought wryly.

She got to her feet and ducked back out the door. There were a couple of men working on a bunker and she called to them. As they approached she asked if they would like to have a weapon and when both nodded, she moved out of their way. In minutes everyone who remained in the village was in front of the weapons hootch, waiting for a turn inside. The men were carrying off the carbines, magazines and ammo. A few took knives. The women and children stole the clothing, sleeping bags and all the food. Lucas found the cache of cigarettes and passed them out. It didn't take the villagers long to empty the hootch, taking even the wood from the ammo crates and the cardboard from the C-ration cartons.

When everything was gone, Lucas left, too. She turned back and smiled. ''Now wage your war,'' she challenged.

She felt satisfied that she had actually done something effective. She didn't delude herself because she knew how much material the Americans had. It would take very little time to replace the stolen gear. A few days at most, but it was time that she could use to convince the villagers they were better off without the gifts of the American soldiers. In the end the soldiers might have to leave.

It was almost dusk when she heard the shout from the eastern side of the village. She was sitting in her hootch, using the last of the fading daylight to write her notes of the day's activities. She had used nearly two pages in her journal explaining how she had engineered the taking of the supplies. Proud that she had found a nonviolent action to accomplish her mission.

When she heard the shout, a cry between anguish and physical pain, she dropped her pen and let it roll to the floor. She leaped up and ran to the doorway stumbling as she jumped to the ground. Then she was up and running. The women and children followed her as she charged through the village until she came to the limits and stopped. The tattered remnants of the patrol staggered in.

She saw dead and wounded and no sign of the Americans. The men who had remained behind ran across the grassy, ash-covered plain to help. She started forward, stopped, afraid that she was violating a taboo and then decided that she could help.

The men set the stretchers at the edge of the village. Some of the wounded men sat up, grinning, pleased that they were home, and pleased that they had wounds to show for their part in the battle. They were going to become heroes because of the fight.

Anxious women passed among them, looking for their men. One stopped at a poncho-wrapped body and peeled the covering back. She was glad to see that it wasn't her husband. But there was a cry behind her, a wail of pain, as that woman recognized the bullet-scarred face of her husband. She collapsed to the dirt, her hands clutched together, screaming in anguish.

Lucas touched the woman's shoulders, trying to pull her away from the dead man, but she refused to move. She fell across his chest, her voice howling. She beat the ground with her tiny fists and refused to be comforted.

The scene was repeated again and again as more women learned that their men were dead. Others, who couldn't find their men, demanded to know what happened or where the rest of the men were. One of the stretcher bearers, his face split by a grin, told how they had slipped away from the main column to hurry home. The rest of the poor men were wandering around the jungle because the big, white soldiers thought it was the thing to do.

Slowly the crowd dispersed. The wounded were taken to their hootches. Lucas made the rounds, looking at the wounds, treating them as best she could with her tiny first-aid kit, although most of the injuries had been dressed already. She was reduced to replacing bandages and pouring more disinfectant onto them.

The bodies were taken away to be prepared for burial. Outside the hootch, Lucas could still hear the crying of the women. She was surprised by the public outpouring of grief. These people were normally more stoic, but she had not witnessed the death ritual since she had arrived. With the death of a relative, it seemed that such a display was demanded.

She finally returned to her own hootch and turned on the battery-powered lantern that she had brought and kept hidden for emergencies. She didn't use it much because the batteries were hard to find in the jungle, but there were some notes and observations that she wanted to make. She found her pen where she had dropped it, then sat on the floor, her back propped against one of the corner posts of the hootch, her journal against her knee. She wrote quickly for several minutes.

A muted pop in the distance stopped her. She turned toward the sound, frowning. The crash of the explosion in the center of the village startled her. She threw her book and pen aside and dived onto her stomach, her hand reaching for the light to shut it off. It was then that the firing broke out around her.

BROMHEAD CURSED THE DARKNESS because it slowed his progress. He had already given up trying to maintain any type of noise discipline because he had to make up time. He was in the front of the column with Beu, who was urging the men to hurry.

They had slashed their way through jungle, no longer worrying about leaving trails and signs for the enemy. They were clearing a path as fast as they could move. They rotated the point men frequently, giving those who had been up front a chance to rest with the rear guard. Although progress was rapid, it took them more than a hour to reach the trail and that put them more than three hours from the village, if the sun was up and they could see what they were doing.

Even the need for speed wasn't sufficient for Bromhead to use any lights. On a dark night on the open sea, a match could be seen for miles and although he was in dense jungle, light had a way of filtering through. It would be suicide to use a light.

Instead they had to feel their way along. The Meos were good, sensing the danger before they reached it, but the night still slowed them. It couldn't be helped.

And all through the march, Bromhead was sure that the NVA and the VC were ahead of them, attacking the village. Too many of the enemy had escaped the ambush. And he knew that the enemy sometimes let large patrols pass to catch them on their return. That was why he never used the same trail twice. But now there was no choice.

So they tried to run up the mountain, moving as fast as they could. Their lungs ached and the breath whistled through their nostrils. They ran when they could, even as the pain spread through their bodies, radiating from their chests. Only when the jungle became too dense did they slow down.

When it seemed that they wouldn't be able to move any faster, the moon rose, bathing the trail in patches of cold, harsh light. Then the pace picked up. Bromhead ran to the head of the column and fell in beside Beu. "We've got to hurry. Make up some time."

Beu turned his head, but said nothing. He increased the pace again.

They had gotten close to the village when they heard the sounds of firing. Beu looked as if he was going to sprint forward, but Bromhead grabbed him and pulled him to the ground. "Wait. Let's recon first. Order the men to stay put."

"The village is being attacked. We must go help."

"Of course," said Bromhead. "But we don't want to rush in there without knowing what is going on. We have to take a look and plan the assault from here."

At that moment there was an explosion from the direction of the village. A mortar round, fired from the north somewhere. Bromhead stared into the jungle, but they were still too far from the village to see anything. They could only hear the sporadic firing. Bursts from AK-47s. Bromhead expected to hear return fire, but it didn't come.

"Colonel Beu," said Bromhead, stressing the use of the rank, "you must convince the men to wait here. Wait for us to determine what is happening in the village. If we just charge into it, a lot of our people are going to die."

Beu nodded but didn't look convinced. He moved to the rear and began talking to his men.

Bromhead was up and moving. He found Gilman. "Nick, we've got to find out what's happening."

"I'm right behind you, Colonel."

Bromhead stepped to Beu and put a hand on his shoulder. "Colonel, you must wait right here. Do not move until we get back."

From the village there was a burst of fire. A lone weapon on full automatic, the sound stitching the night like a cloth being ripped.

"Nick," said Bromhead. He nodded to the right.

"Right with you."

Together they ran into the jungle, following the path. After ten minutes they slowed. The village wasn't far away now and Bromhead didn't want to accidentally find the enemy. They left the trail, skirting it, following it at the edge of the jungle. They came to the tree line and surveyed the grassy plain where the village stood.

There were a couple of fires burning. Hootches had been set ablaze by tracers or red-hot shrapnel. White smoke poured from one of them, looking gray in the moonlight. There seemed to be a body lying in the dirt at the foot of a notched log. There was no sign of the villagers or the enemy. It was quiet. Not even the dogs were barking.

For a horrifying moment Bromhead was sure that the villagers had all been captured and led away. Then in the flickering firelight, a shadow leaped up and ran to the south. It dived under one of the hootches and didn't reappear.

From the north came a short burst from an AK-47. The green tracers ripped through the dark. Bromhead sought their point of origin. The muzzle-flashes winked among the trees. He touched Gilman on the shoulder and pointed. Gilman nodded.

They pulled back deeper into the jungle, stopping near the trunk of a gigantic tree. Bromhead put his lips next to Gilman's ear. "Let's see what's happening over there."

They continued still deeper into the jungle, working their way north, being careful of the vegetation. Bromhead cautiously placed his heel on the ground in front of him and slowly rotated his foot forward until he could shift his weight to that leg. It was a tedious way to walk, but it prevented him from making noise. He came to the trail, crouched for a moment watching it, then crossed to the other side. Somewhere the VC or the NVA had to have a guard, he figured. Someone to warn the others that reinforcements for the villagers were on the way.

Bromhead waited until Gilman came close. "Find their rear guard and eliminate it."

Gilman nodded. He slung his carbine and drew the Kabar Combat Knife. He grinned, his teeth flashing white in the blackness of the night. Then he disappeared.

Bromhead stared after him and then dropped to the ground. He crawled forward on his belly using his elbows and knees, the carbine clutched in his hands. Once across the trail and safely hidden in the bush, he got to his feet. He followed the edge of the jungle, all senses alert. Dropping to the ground again, he crept forward. He could feel the wetness of the jungle floor seeping through his uniform but ignored the cold, clammy feeling.

Ahead of him he heard the bolt of a rifle slam forward. He turned toward the sound and saw two men standing next to a palm tree. One of them was leaning on it, holding his rifle by the barrel, the butt on the ground. The other was aiming at something in the village, but did not fire.

Farther to the west, there came a burst as one of the NVA soldiers emptied an entire magazine. Bromhead saw the green tracers disappear into the thatch of a hootch. Moments later fire began to spread upward from the point of impact.

Bromhead continued to move to the west. He passed the two men, saw another crouched near a bush and then found still more of them. They seemed to be fairly casual. No one was actually watching the village or shooting at it with any regularity. Suddenly he realized what they were doing. They were holding the villagers in place, waiting for the rest of the men to arrive. The NVA expected Beu's men to run up the trail, and as they entered the ville, the enemy would open fire. Two squads would be able to set up a devastating cross fire. He hoped that Gilman wouldn't find a guard along the trail. It would be best to slip away without taking out the guard.

GILMAN KNEW EXACTLY what he had to do. He turned to the east and crawled off slowly, his eyes moving, watching the dark shadows around him, searching for a flicker of motion. His knife was clasped in his right hand, the tip off the ground, pointing upward.

He paralleled the trail for several yards, stopped and listened. Then, suddenly to the left, he heard a muffled cough. It was almost inaudible and if he hadn't been listening he would never have heard it.

He turned his head slowly, searching with the corner of his eyes. At first there was nothing to see. The bushes, trees and ferns of the jungle had blended into a single black smear. And then there was a flicker of motion. The enemy soldier took form, his outline barely visible in the surrounding jungle.

Gilman grinned, retreating a couple of feet. He stood, his eyes roaming the area where the enemy soldier was standing. Gilman spotted him again, saw that the man was watching the village, occasionally glancing at the trail but obviously not expecting trouble from that direction.

Gilman moved forward slowly, being careful where he put his feet. He reached out with his left hand, feeling his way along until he was only a few feet from the enemy. Gilman let the man look at the trail and as his head pivoted toward the village, Gilman struck.

He stepped forward, grabbed the man under the chin, lifting the head as he pulled back. Gilman went down on his left knee. His right came up, striking the man in the spine. As the man fell against the fulcrum of his knee, Gilman's knife flashed. He heard the quiet whisper as the knife slashed the tender skin of the throat. The enemy spasmed and bucked as his blood washed over Gilman's hand in a warm flow. Gilman felt the man's mouth working as he tried to scream a warning to his friends but there was only a soft gurgle.

Gilman moved back, stretching the man out and then jamming his knife up under the ribs to pierce the heart. The soldier's muscles went rigid as he drummed his heels into the rotting vegetation making a quiet, rustling sound, and then he relaxed immediately.

Gilman grabbed the enemy's rifle and slipped deeper into the jungle as a voice called out in Vietnamese. He heard the soft steps of someone approaching and realized it was a second guard. Gilman moved forward, closing on the body. Through a gap in the vegetation he saw the dark outline of another NVA soldier.

As that man crouched over the body of his dead friend, Gilman attacked. He reached around the man, his hand over the mouth and pinching the nose shut. As he lifted the enemy's head, he struck with the knife, cutting the throat with such force that he nearly severed the head from the body. The blood spattered the surrounding jungle, sounding like a morning rain on the broad-leaf plants. Gilman felt the warm liquid splash him as he lowered the dead man to the ground.

Again he stripped the weapon from the body, and cut free the chest pouch for the spare ammo. He wiped the blood from the blade, and sheathed his knife. He looped one of the AKs over his shoulder and held the other in his hands. If he had to shoot, it would sound like one of the enemy taking a potshot at the village.

He started walking until he found the trail. Here he crouched near a fern that dripped water onto his shoulder. Several minutes later he saw Bromhead cross the trail, and moved toward him. Together they slipped away from the jungle and once clear Gilman said, "I got two of them."

"Shit," said Bromhead. "I really wish you hadn't done that now."

Gilman was confused. "But you told me to get them."

"I know. Maybe the VC won't find the bodies before we get back. I think it would be easier to get in if they don't know how close we are."

"You have a plan, then?" asked Gilman.

"Sure. We're going to attack one of the enemy squads from the rear and run right into the middle of the village. We can't get involved in a long firefight outside because we used so much of our ammo in the ambush. Once in the village, we can resupply from the supply hut. If we do it right, we'll catch these guys by surprise."

"Yes, sir. If we do it right."

"You're such a pessimist," said Bromhead.

Gilman nodded and realized that Bromhead couldn't see the gesture in the dark. "Yes, sir," he said. "With very good reason, too."

9

THE JUNGLES OF LAOS
EAST OF THE MEO
VILLAGE

It took forty minutes to get back to the main column, have Beu translate the plan for the men, and make sure they all understood that no one could act on his own. An individual mistake could kill everyone in the village. They had to be patient, but once the battle started, they would have to be ferocious.

Each of the men complained about the slow pace as they returned to the village. They wanted to hurry, but each remembered that the problem had come about because they had refused to listen to Bromhead. He had warned them and they had ignored it. Now the village was in jeopardy.

They left the trail short of the destination and moved through the jungle. Bromhead knew the Meos were there around him, but he could no longer see or hear them. They were quieter than the wind in the trees, slipping in and out of the shadows like spirits. Thirty men had suddenly vanished as they moved through the forest.

Then they were behind the VC and NVA. Bromhead, who hugged the ground, could see one of the enemy soldiers, an AK clutched loosely in his hands, facing the village. The fires had almost gone out, some of the huts reduced to glowing embers scattered by the light breeze blowing up the mountainside.

Bromhead checked the safety on his M-1 carbine, making sure that it was off. Slowly he got to his knees and then to his feet, crouching among the shadows. He raised his weapon and sighted over the top of the barrel as he had learned to do in night-firing training. When he was looking at the enemy soldier, he froze, took a breath and let half of it out. He wanted to glance to the right and left, but knew the gesture was useless in the dark. He forced his concentration back to the single enemy he could see. His finger tightened on the trigger until the weapon fired. Bromhead lost sight of the soldier in the flash from his muzzle, but he heard the round impact. The man screamed in pain and disappeared.

At that moment everyone was up and running. Gilman was beside Bromhead, firing his M-1 from the hip as they advanced on the village. Shooting broke out to the left, the dark jungle sparkling with the muzzle-flashes like woods loaded with lightning bugs. Green tracers whipped out, some of them striking the ground and bouncing high.

Bromhead ignored them, his eyes focused on the village. He ran toward the corner of a hootch and dived for cover there. He rolled through a puddle of water, coating himself with mud. As he got to his knees, a bullet struck the hootch near his head, showering him with debris. He spun, saw the enemy soldier and aimed. He squeezed off a quick three rounds, but the man kept coming. Bromhead aimed and fired again. This time his adversary went down. His weapon flew into the air as he disappeared into the grass.

Now Bromhead looked into the hootch, but in the darkened interior, he could see nothing. He couldn't tell if there was anyone in there or not. He called out in French, but there was no reply.

Firing increased all around. Individual weapons shooting on full auto, the strings of detonations of grenade and mortar combining into a drawn out explosion. There was shouting as the Meos called to each other, searching for their families.

Bromhead ran from the hootch in a crouch, moving toward the center of the village. He leaped up the notched log and into the weapons hootch, rolling on his shoulder. He wanted to get a crate of grenades and one of hand flares. A few of those over the village would give them an advantage, but the hootch looked empty. He scrambled around, feeling with his hand, but found nothing. He risked using his flashlight momentarily and saw that the only things left were a few scraps of lumber and some paper. Everything was gone, including the spare ammunition.

He dived back out, rolling away from the hootch. He stared into the distance. In the moonlight, and the flickering of a newly started fire, he could see people running. Men were carrying M-1s or AK-47s. Enough of his own men had AKs that he didn't dare shoot at anyone until he identified the target better.

From the east, where the path lead into the jungle and then down the mountain, came a burst of firing. A line of tracers from a Russian RPD stitched the night. Bromhead marked the position. Normally he would toss grenades, but he only had one. Besides, without support, he'd never be able to get it.

The firing continued, the bullets ripping through the village. Bromhead crawled forward, his face nearly pressed to the ground. He worked his way under one of the huts until he was against the support leg. He aimed his carbine at the muzzle-flashes of the RPD. He pulled the trigger rapidly until the bolt locked back and his weapon stopped firing. As he rolled to his right, he hit the magazine release. The magazine dropped to the ground, and he slapped another one home, worked the bolt and aimed. The RPD had stopped shooting for a moment.

And then it opened up again, the flashes pointed straight at Bromhead. Green tracers apparently the size of basketballs came at him. Somehow they seemed larger than those fired at another target.

He hugged the ground, pressing his face into the soft, moist earth. He could smell the dirt. Could taste it. And above him, the bullets drilled into the wooden floor. He could hear them splitting the air, sounding like angry insects.

Without a conscious thought, he raised his rifle again. Two hundred yards away, he could see the muzzle-flashes of the enemy. He chose a spot at the center and began shooting. Feeling the recoil of the weapon as it slammed back into his shoulder. He could smell the cordite. It was an acrid stink that reminded him of Fourth of July firecrackers tossed around the front yard.

When the bolt locked back, he didn't bother to reload. The firing was tapering off. There were no AKs firing now. Even the RPD had fallen silent. Some of his men were still pouring rounds into the jungle, but there was nothing coming back.

Bromhead crawled from his hiding place and reloaded his weapon. It was his last magazine. If the enemy decided to rush them, there would be some shooting and then it would all be hand-to-hand. But the enemy had broken the contact. They had decided that the battle was over and withdrawn. Bromhead knew that it was only a momentary respite. They would be back as soon as they had regrouped.

He pulled at the camouflage flap on his watch and saw that it was nearly three. It would be light in less than three hours, closer to two. If the VC and NVA held true to form, they wouldn't launch an assault with so little darkness left. They would wait until the following evening.

Of course, that was the tactic the VC used in South Vietnam where the Americans could call on air power to help them. A hundred helicopters carrying six hundred soldiers could land within minutes of a cry for help. The tactics in Laos, where help didn't exist, might be different.

Bromhead turned and ran back to the weapons hootch. He found Gilman, Hansen and a couple of the Meos standing there. As Beu approached, Bromhead started to demand an answer, realized that Beu probably didn't know anything about it, either. He lowered his voice and asked Beu if he knew what had happened.

The headman didn't know. He told Bromhead the men wanted to find their families. They had searched the village and the only thing they had found were three dead men and a dead woman.

"All right," said Bromhead, "we need to get some security out now. Colonel Beu, we'll need ten men. Five to go with Major Gilman and five with Major Hansen."

"Men find families first."

"No, Colonel, we get security out first. If the Communists come back and surprise us, we'll all die. We get the security set and then we try to find the families."

"We find families first," insisted Beu.

"Colonel," said Bromhead patiently, "I don't want to have to say this, but you saw what happened when you ignored my advice. This didn't have to happen."

Beu lowered his eyes and stared at the dirt. "First security and then we search."

"Good." Bromhead clapped Beu on the shoulder. "You find the men who will go on patrol. Might I suggest that the family men be excluded if we can fill out the patrol without them."

As Beu turned to select his men, Bromhead called, "Major Gilman?"

"Here, sir."

"You get the thankless job of going back into the jungle on patrol. Near the path I would guess, about a klick or two out."

"Great."

"Yeah, I thought you'd like that. We'll keep the patrol out until first light."

"Major Hansen, get on the radio if you can find it, and report in. Tell them we need a medic in here. There are wounded that must have medical assistance."

"Yes, sir."

"Then we—"

He was interrupted by a shout from the south side of the village. Bromhead could see nothing except that the tiny force was beginning to melt away. More shouting and cries of joy. Bromhead followed the crowd, and stopped. The missing villagers were pouring out of the jungle, running across the grass toward their homes. Some of the men dropped their weapons and rushed out to meet them.

Bromhead pushed his way through the knot of people who were jabbering happily to one another. He found Beu and told them, "We need to get the people out of the open."

Beu looked at him, distracted. He held one wife under one arm and a second under the other. He was grinning widely. Standing to the rear, in the shadows, was the woman that he had given to Bromhead during a noon meal. She was confused, looking from her husband, the headman and then to Bromhead, wondering which man she should run to.

"We can hold the reunion in the village, Colonel," said Bromhead, glancing at the woman, but giving her no indication about his intentions. "There are things that have to be done." At the edge of the group stood Jane Lucas. She was dressed in khaki, looking a little pale, although it was hard to tell in the moonlight.

As the people began moving slowly into the village, Bromhead turned from the Meo woman and approached Lucas. "You okay?" he asked.

"Okay?" she repeated.

"You hurt?"

"No," she said, shaking her head. "No, I'm not hurt. Scared. I'm plenty scared."

Bromhead reached out as if to put an arm around her shoulder and then let his hand drop to his side when he felt her tense. He was still confused by the woman. She seemed to be strong-willed and able to take care of herself. Not everyone could go running around a hostile jungle and survive. As they walked toward the ville, Bromhead shot a glance over his shoulder. The Meo woman was following him at a respectable distance.

"Let me help you," said Bromhead, again reaching out to Lucas.

"No," she said. "I'll be all right." She was silent for a moment, walking along with the crowd, Bromhead beside her. Then she said, "They didn't even warn us. They just started shooting. All we could do was run from them."

"They didn't sweep through the village?" asked Bromhead.

"No. Stayed in the jungle, shooting. Killed some people. Wounded some. Just shot them down with no warning. Nothing."

"Wounded. How badly?"

"We took care of them," she said, almost as if her mind was elsewhere. "It was like they wanted us to leave the village. Like they had some plan."

"You're sure they didn't enter the village."

"They stayed in the jungle and shot at us," she repeated.

Bromhead rubbed a hand over his face. He could feel the combined stubble from not shaving, dirt from crawling through the mud, and the grime from firing his weapon. He also realized how tried he was becoming. His eyes burned as if he had been standing in a smoke-filled room for hours. He felt slightly lightheaded, and he had an uncontrollable urge to laugh, but there was nothing funny.

They stopped walking when they came to the weapons hootch. He noticed the blank look on her face. Her eyes were wide and white, giving the impression that there was no pupil in them. She turned to him and spoke. "They just started shooting. Didn't matter that you and the soldiers weren't here. Didn't matter that the majority of the people were women and children. They just started shooting at us."

Bromhead reached down and took her hand. "I'm not one to say that I told you so, but I did warn you about the Communists. They're not interested in leaving the people alone. Communists think that everyone was put on the planet for the benefit of the state. If the people don't respond to the state, then they're eliminated."

She shook her head. It was as if she didn't hear a word that Bromhead had said. "Just started shooting."

"Jane." Bromhead tried to jerk her attention back to reality. "Jane. Do you know what happened to our equipment?"

She looked at him for a moment, as if confused by his words, and then said in a voice devoid of emotion, "I gave it away."

"You what?" Bromhead was unable to believe what he had heard. He stared at her. "Gave it away? To whom? Why in the hell would you do something that stupid?" He felt like vomiting. His stomach twisted and churned.

She lifted a hand and waved it. "I gave it to everyone here. Told them to take what they wanted and kept at it until everything was gone."

"Shit! Why?"

"I don't know," she said, whining. "I thought . . . I just thought that it would show you. I thought . . ."

Bromhead was seized with the urge to shake her. To slap her. He started to speak, his voice filled with anger, stopped and started again, forcing himself to talk in a calm tone. "Why would you do that? You've put us all in jeopardy."

She shrugged helplessly. "I didn't know. I thought it would make you leave. That everything could go back to the way it was before you came." As she looked at him, her eyes filled with tears. "I just wanted these people to be left alone."

That didn't satisfy Bromhead. He still wanted to slap her but didn't. He wanted to shove his hand through the wall, wanted to kick something. The rage burned through him, threatening to consume him. His fists clenched and his muscles tightened until they ached. He took a half-step toward her, and then stopped himself. Standing there, ready to attack her, he forced himself to be calm. He forced himself to retreat. Through clenched teeth, he asked, "Only to people in this village?"

"Yes. I suppose so. I guess. It's all still here somewhere."

"Then all I have to do is talk to Beu and convince him to have the people bring it back," said Bromhead. He felt the cloud lift because the equipment could be recovered. "We can still salvage something from this. Maybe it'll work out after all."

"They kept shooting," she repeated, ignoring him.

Bromhead pushed her to the notched log and made her sit down. "You stay here," he ordered. "Don't move and don't think. I'll be back."

He left her sitting there and headed toward Gilman. Approaching the big Marine, he said, "Let's get some sentries out, then you organize your patrol. Tell the sentries to fire twice if they spot anything and then get the hell back here."

"They could jump the gun. Shoot at shadows," said Gilman.

"That's better than having them afraid to do anything and having the enemy sneak up on us."

"I'll get on it, Colonel."

"One thing you'd better know. Lucas told the villagers they could have anything in our hootch they wanted. Cleaned us out. That's why I'm sending you out like this. I'm going to try to recover our stuff."

"Great, Colonel. Any more good news I should know about?"

"That about covers it."

As Gilman disappeared, searching for recruits for his patrol and guards, Hansen said, "Colonel, I've been on the radio to our control."

"Jesus, I wanted to talk to you before you did that."

"Yes, sir, sorry, sir. I didn't think. Besides, we'd already missed a check-in and they've been broadcasting to us. They were madder than hell."

"What's so fucking important?" said Bromhead. "Christ! Why does everything have to be so hard?"

"We're being pulled out," said Hansen.

"What?" Bromhead was incredulous.

"Yes, sir. Apparently there has been some flack on the home front and the pressure has caused the President to deny that there are any American combat troops in either Cambodia or Laos. Because of all that, they're pulling all the teams. We're to get out as quickly as possible."

Bromhead took a deep breath. "We can't go now. How the fuck are we supposed to get all the equipment out?" He wiped a hand across his forehead and thought about paper-pushers and university liberals. Neither group seemed to understand the nature of war, but each group kept acting as if they did.

"We're going to be pulled out by helicopter the day after tomorrow." Hansen glanced up at the lightening sky. "Or rather tomorrow. In the meantime, we are to do nothing that would cause any kind of a ripple."

Now Bromhead smiled. "You mean like ambushing the NVA in Laos and beating off a Communist attack?"

"They didn't go into specifics, sir, but I think you've hit the nail on the head."

Bromhead turned and walked back toward the weapons hootch, Hansen right beside him. Lucas hadn't moved. She was sitting with her head down, staring at the dirt. Bromhead halted and said to Hansen, "Okay, why don't you get some sleep? In about an hour, we're going to have to get up and put in a long day."

"Yes, sir," said Hansen.

As Hansen stepped around Lucas and ducked into the hootch, Bromhead had the urge to kick her butt. He squashed the feeling and said as calmly as he could, "Got to ask you a favor."

Her voice seemed to come from a long way. She didn't look up as she said, "Yes?"

"Since you gave our equipment away, do you think you could get most of it back? I think the Communists are going to return. This time they're not going to be satisfied with shooting into the village, and killing or wounding a few people. They're going to sweep through here and kill everyone they can before they burn the village to the ground."

"Then we have to get out." Her voice shook.

"No, I think that if we put up a good fight and drive them off, it'll be better. If we run for it, they'll follow and we won't have a big enough lead, especially with the sick, wounded and the kids. But if we fight, it'll be a week or more before they come back. Give everyone a chance to get out."

Lucas stood up. She started to speak, stopped and then started again. "I don't know if this is your fault or not. Your fault for being here. Maybe if you hadn't come this would have happened anyway. Maybe it wouldn't. I don't know anymore." She stopped talking for a moment, looked up at him and then added, "But I know what we have to do now. Yes, I'll see what I can do to get the equipment returned."

"Then I'll give you the good news. In a little more than twenty-four hours, my men and I will be on a chopper flying out of here. We'll take our weapons of war with us." He stressed the last sentence, but it was lost on Jane Lucas.

"What about the people here?" she asked.

"That's the one thing that everyone seems to overlook. We blow in and provide some aid, train the people to fight the Communists and then we blow out with no thought of how that will affect them. Suddenly we're a political potato and the politicians don't give a fuck about the people. The people may want it or maybe they just don't know how to refuse it. Makes no difference what the people think once we're in. We owe it to them to see it through to the end, but the politicians in Washington refuse to understand that. We owe these people and can't just leave them."

"You have orders," said Lucas.

"So, we tell them to get the hell out of here and leave them as much of the materiel as we can. Leave the weapons because we owe them that much, at the very least." Bromhead shook his head. "I don't understand this. Not at all. I don't know what these idiots are thinking about, but the last thing on the list has to be the people."

"What are you going to do?"

"Spend the day trying to prepare for the attack that is going to come tonight. Buy as much time as I can for these people, and then get on the chopper to go home."

"Jack," she said, "I didn't understand what you were trying to do, or what was going on here. All I saw was that you were bringing your war to these people who didn't want a thing to do with it. But I was wrong. I didn't understand the mind of the enemy." She stopped suddenly as she realized what she was saying. She let her eyes drop again and continued. "I don't know if you're right, or I'm right, or anything now, but if there is anything that I can do to help you, please let me know."

"Right now, all we need is to get our equipment back." He turned, thought for a moment. "It might not be safe for you here anymore. Maybe you had better get out with us."

"You mean the people here would harm me?"

"No. I mean the Communists would have a field day if they captured you. Have you sign documents confessing to everything from spying to using poison gas."

"You can't be serious."

"The mere fact that you're an American puts you in jeopardy. Your affiliation with a university won't do you any good. Even if you don't go out with us, you'd better think about getting out quickly."

She sat quietly for a moment, as if thinking about her options. She looked around the village, hard to see in the fading moonlight, and the early glow of the rising sun. She shook her head. "I'll have to think about this. My work is here."

"You can find other work," said Bromhead, "if you're still alive. You can let me know sometime tomorrow."

Lucas stood and brushed at the seat of her skirt. "What are you going to do?"

"Catch some sleep and then get up at dawn to see if I can get ready for the Communists."

"Good luck."

"Yeah. I think we're going to need it."

10

THE MEO VILLAGE

The light seeping into the weapons hootch woke Bromhead just after dawn. It wasn't very bright out, and Bromhead had only been asleep for a little more than an hour, but it was enough. He rolled to his side, groaned and sat up.

Behind him, almost touching him, was the Meo woman. She had slipped closer to him as he had slept. For a moment she didn't move, then she rolled over and stared up at him.

Hansen was sleeping on the bare floor, his hand clutching the handset of the radio. He was snoring quietly. Bromhead decided to let him sleep a little longer.

Bromhead got to his feet, saw dark for a moment because he had stood up too quickly, and closed his eyes. He pressed a hand to his head, took a deep breath and stood still. When the dizziness passed, he moved to the door, then glanced back at the woman. He smiled at her, ducked, and looked into the early morning mist.

Unlike the lowlands, the mornings were chilly. There was a wispy fog rising from the jungle, some of it drifting into the open, making it look as if the trees had caught fire. Bromhead inhaled deeply, felt the cool air sear his throat and he nearly coughed.

Then, on the ground near the notched log he saw a couple of crates. Bromhead dropped to the earth and noticed that there were over a dozen boxes sitting there, too. Lucas had been true to her word. Already the villagers were returning the equipment.

One of the boxes held C-rations. It hadn't been opened. Bromhead crouched near it, levered a hand under one of the cardboard flaps and ripped upward. He looked at the twenty-four meals and pulled one out.

As he opened the scrambled eggs, Gilman materialized out of the mist, saw the boxes and said, "You rear area commandoes have all the luxury. Sitting around eating tasty meals why we poor soldiers have to hump the bush."

"Here, grab something to eat."

Gilman leaned his weapon against the log and knelt near the C-rations.

"Something you don't know," said Bromhead. "We've been recalled. Sometime tomorrow they're sending a chopper to pull us out."

Gilman selected one of the meals. "I'll eat the beans and franks, then. No sense in saving them now."

Bromhead shoved the plastic spoon in to the eggs and set the can down. He wasn't sure if he could eat any more of them or not. He looked at Gilman. "You're taking it remarkably calmly."

"Figured that we'd be out of here quickly. This kind of mission makes too many of the bureaucrats antsy. They think about the unconventional nature of it and then about their careers, and they back down. Came a little quicker than I expected, though."

"How you feeling?" asked Bromhead.

"You mean, am I tired? Hell, yes. Can I go without sleep a little longer? Hell, yes."

Bromhead grinned. "No, I meant your other problem."

Gilman sat down and used his P-38 to open the C-ration can. When he had it opened, he spooned out a bite. "Hurts like hell to piss. My arms and legs hurt and I'm hotter than hell. Other than that, I'd like to throw up."

"Then the good news. Should be a medic on the choppers. Get you a massive shot of penicillin and solve your problem."

"That'll be a relief," said Gilman. "Those damned pills weren't doing much for me."

"Tell you what," said Bromhead. "Why don't you catch a nap now and join us later? Hansen and I'll get the people started on what needs to be done here."

Bromhead picked up his eggs, looked at the sickly yellow concoction and took another bite. At that moment, Lucas, escorted by two men carrying a long crate, appeared.

"Told you I'd get your stuff back," she said.

"You get any sleep?" he asked, noticing that she was still wearing her khaki safari outfit.

"Figured I could get enough after this is over. Had a lot to do."

"As a point of interest," said Bromhead, "you've gotten the right stuff back to us. Those boxes of ammo are going to be as precious as gold before the day is over."

"What do we do now?" she asked.

"As soon as everyone is awake, we organize work details. If Beu agrees to abandon the village after the battle is over, then we turn some of the hootches into bunkers. We make a couple for the families to hide in. I doubt that Charlie or the NVA will bring anything bigger than a mortar and a couple of thick logs will protect the civilians. We get a line of defense established and then wait for the bad guys."

"This will work?"

"Naturally," said Bromhead. He was amazed at how completely her attitude had turned. One day it seemed that she couldn't stand the sight of him and the next, she was doing everything she could to help. Maybe it was seeing the enemy standing in the jungle sniping at innocent women and children. Maybe it was the way the Communists responded to the presence of the Americans. No talk, no discussion, just a volley from the jungle. Seeing something like that could change anyone's mind.

"Colonel," said Gilman, getting to his feet, "I'm going to catch some sleep."

"Okay."

As he disappeared into the hootch, Lucas moved closer and lowered her voice. "I've been thinking about what you said last night. About getting out of here when you go. I think you're right."

"You'll be going with us?"

"If you'll let me."

Bromhead jammed the spoon into the remains of the eggs and set the can aside. "When the chopper arrives, you just get on it. I doubt the pilots or the crew will say anything. All hell will break loose in Vietnam, but then you'll be there and it'll be someone else's problem."

"You don't seem too concerned about it."

"Lady, it's the least of the problems staring at us right now."

"I guess you're right. What should we do?"

Bromhead pushed the can back into the box and dumped the remains of the meal into the carton. He dusted his hands together. "Right now I'm going to see Beu and start the ball rolling."

"Mind if I tag along?"

"Please do."

FETTERMAN SAT IN THE DIM recesses of the commo bunker, his feet propped on an empty ammo crate, sipping coffee and waiting for a reply to his latest message. During the night he had listened to a wide range of radio reports, some from artillerymen using their weapons to interdict the Ho Chi Minh Trail, some from helicopter pilots as they flew over the area and others from grunts stuck deep in the jungle.

He had heard the coded transmissions directed at Captain Bromhead and his team in Laos. With growing apprehension, he had waited for an acknowledgment, and then had gone to find Gerber. Together they waited until someone on Bromhead's team had responded. During that time they had tried, without success, to find an Army aviation unit that would knowingly cross the border to drop strikers into the jungle. One or two commanders said they would check with higher headquarters and get back.

Finally Fetterman heard it all. Bromhead's radio operator using both code and transmitting in the clear, told of the assault on the village. Although Fetterman's first reaction was to rush in to help, by the time he had the information he needed, it was clear that the attack had failed.

Now he waited for the aviation unit commanders to call back with a detailed listing of the air assets that were available. He watched the green boxes, their tiny lights glowing, and listened to the crackle of static. There were a couple of messages directed to the Special Forces camp, but those were logged by the young, stocky, sergeant who sat near the radios, dozing in the cool darkness of the bunker.

Gerber made his way down the wooden steps, the leather of his boots scraping on the coating of dust. He stopped at the entrance and blinked. "Tony?"

"Over here, Captain."

Gerber made his way through the dimness, missing the map table shoved against one wall, barely visible in the half-light filtering in. He stepped around a wooden folding chair. "What's the word?"

"One called back and said that a cross-border op was out of the question unless orders were issued in Saigon. I suggested that we'd be retrieving a unit of American soldiers and he said he was sorry but orders were orders."

Gerber nodded. "Can't blame him for that."

"Well, sir," said Fetterman, "I believe he'd want to do anything he could to help other Americans. Hell, sir, I would."

"Yes, well, not everyone feels that way. Some men are more concerned with careers and family than they are about unknown soldiers caught in trouble somewhere else. I don't understand it, either."

At that moment the radio squawked and the message started. Both Fetterman and Gerber looked toward it.

"Zulu Six, Zulu Six, this is Vampire Six."

Gerber crossed to the radio where the NCO handed him the mike. "This is Zulu Six."

"Roger, Six. Be advised that I will be able to supply seven aircraft, available after fifteen thirty hours."

"Roger. Will the ships be on standby here?"

"Negative. They will remain on station."

Gerber turned and snapped his fingers at the NCO. "Where is Vampire Six located?"

The NCO pulled a small booklet out of the open safe and flipped through it. "Vampire Six is the CO of the 158th Assault Helicopter Company at Kontum."

"Shit. Not close enough." He pressed the button on the mike. "Request aircraft standby here."

"Negative, Zulu Six. I repeat. Negative."

"Roger," snapped Gerber. "How long are the aircraft available?"

"You can have the ships for thirty hours."

"Roger. Thanks." Gerber handed the mike back to the NCO.

"Better than nothing," said Fetterman. "Gives a little breathing space."

"Except that with those helicopters standing by at Kontum, it'll be over an hour before we could get off the ground here. Hell, considering the relaying of the messages, getting the crews out and the people loaded, it could take two hours and we'd still not be on the way."

"So what do we do?" asked Fetterman.

"Get with Blanchfeld and have him request aviation support but not give any destinations. Have the backup ships available and see if we can get them to stand by here."

"Why?" asked Fetterman.

"If we've got the people on the ships and kept directing the flight lead, we might be able to sneak across the border."

Fetterman grinned. "You really think the pilot won't know where he is or that he's operating near the border?"

"No, I guess not. Might be able to slip a klick into Laos by accident, but never far enough to help Johnnie."

"You mean Jack."

"Whatever," said Gerber with a flip of his hand. "Once we're on board and heading out, I doubt they'll abort the mission. Besides, most of those chopper pilots are crazy anyway."

"So what do we do now?"

Gerber rubbed his eyes. They felt like someone had thrown a handful of sand into them. "Right now I suggest we grab some breakfast and then see what else we can arrange. Especially for tonight."

IT TOOK ALMOST NO TIME to get the work parties started. Beu agreed that the village would have to be abandoned after the battle because the Communists would just return with a larger, better equipped force.

Bromhead explained how he planned to use the logs from the floors of the huts and the stilts for makeshift bunkers. He told Beu he wanted a large one in the middle of the village for the families. And they would finish those on the perimeter, use them for the primary defense and then retreat as the ground attack started.

Beu wasn't interested in the tactics. He called his men together to give them their instructions. Once that was done, the working parties spread out, some of them taking axes into the jungle to fell more trees.

Everyone worked quickly. By noon they had completed all the bunkers on the corners of the village and erected one on each side between them. They were fairly makeshift affairs of shallow holes covered by logs, but they would protect the defenders from mortars.

Then Bromhead began burning off the grass around the village to deny the enemy that cover. Others were busy building bunkers for the families, erecting a second line of defense, and stocking the entire perimeter with weapons and ammunition. They sighted a couple of machine guns along the most likely routes of assault where they could support one another.

There was a short break for lunch. Hansen handed out the C-rations for everyone since they figured they wouldn't need them much longer. The Meo woman hovered in the background, saying nothing, but trying to anticipate Bromhead's needs. She was never far from him and refused the C-ration meal that Hansen tried to give her. As the people finished eating, he collected the cans and stored them, sure that someone would find a use for them later.

Throughout the afternoon, they strengthened the defenses. They built hidden punji pits to channel the assaults. They set up some grenades in the cans that Hansen had saved, added trip wires so that the enemy would jerk the grenade free to explode. Using several of the claymore mines, they rigged a couple of booby traps inside the trees where the enemy might assemble, then set the others facing across the grass to be command detonated. These were mechanical ambushes designed to frighten the enemy and alert the defenders of the VC's approach. They also created a couple of false bunkers to draw enemy fire and booby trapped those.

In the late afternoon Bromhead set up several listening posts with instructions to return by moonrise if they had heard nothing or had seen nothing. He sent Gilman and three men down the path and told them to wait there for a couple of hours. Gilman suggested another mechanical ambush, grenades in cans and a claymore rigged to a trip wire. Bromhead agreed.

Finally, Bromhead realized that there was nothing else to be done. There was no time left and it was getting dark. He suggested that Beu have the families enter the bunkers in the middle of the village. Bromhead asked Beu to instruct his people to stay put and not stray too far. If an attack came, it would be swift, and the people caught in the open would be in great danger.

With the setting of the sun, Bromhead stopped roaming. First he went to the weapons hootch where the Meo woman waited patiently. Bromhead sent her to wait with the rest of the women and children in the family bunkers. As he stepped into the cooling evening, he saw Lucas. She glanced at him, started around a corner and then turned back.

"You have a minute to talk?" she asked.

The defenses were as close to being ready as he could make them. Gilman was still out, listening for the enemy, and Hansen had reported their status to their control. Now it was up to the enemy to either attack them, or to avoid them.

He nodded. "I have some time."

She came closer, halted and looked up at him. "I've spent my whole life in school," she said. "From high school to college and into the graduate program. Everything I've learned has been from books. Some of the books were accurate. I studied the influence of alcohol on our society and could sit in a bar and predict the behavior of the people.''

''This is fascinating,'' said Bromhead, ''but do you have a point?''

''Too much of what I learned was the ideal. If everyone did *this*, there would be no more war, or poverty, or murder. If we outlawed handguns, the murder rate would drop...''

''That's a load of horse—''

''I realize that now,'' she said, cutting him off. ''I realize that the use of handguns in murder is a symptom. Eliminating the gun will not eliminate the cause of the murder.''

Bromhead glanced around.

''Please,'' she said. ''Bear with me. This is very difficult for me. I've thought about it all day and I have to admit that many of the things I thought were true are not. I'm trying to tell you that I think you might be right.''

''Right, Miss Lucas? Right about what?''

She looked away, at the ground and then at the notched log leading up into the weapons hootch. ''Right about what you said. This war isn't going to end because I don't like it. Those men last night...'' She shook her head. ''They didn't ask questions, they just started shooting. The Communists talk about equality but if you don't believe...'' She shrugged.

''The difference,'' said Bromhead, ''is that we don't come in shooting. We try to show the people what they need to know to make their lives a little more pleasant.'' Now he stopped because he realized that he sounded like a propaganda film.

''Anyway,'' said Lucas, ''I'm sorry for all I've said and done.''

''Thank you for that, Jane.''

''I'm not saying that I think war is the way to solve our problems, but I've seen some things here that make me wonder. Maybe there is a good reason for...'' Again she was stumped, almost as if unsure of what she now felt. She realized that she wasn't saying what she wanted to. Finally she just said, "Anyway, I'm sorry for what I said."

"Well, no harm done," said Bromhead. "I think you'd better join the families in their bunker. It's going to be a long night."

As she turned to go, Bromhead moved to the bunker that guarded the path leading into the jungle and crawled in. The disadvantage was that the low firing port made it hard to watch the jungle. He gave it up and crawled out. At first he lay on top of the bunker and then realized it would be a target for the enemy gunners. Instead he crouched beside it, using his binoculars to search the jungle, looking for signs that the enemy was near.

As he lay there he realized just how hot and tired he was. He could feel the sweat dripping down his face and along his sides. He swiped at his forehead with the sleeve of his fatigues, then took a deep breath. His eyes felt sore. It was nothing that three days of sleep wouldn't cure. In two days he would be in Saigon, could take a hot bath and lie naked on clean sheets. The image danced in his head and in the fantasy he could see Jane Lucas enter the room dressed in nothing except a tiny towel wrapped around her waist.

He shook the thoughts from his mind and concentrated on the task before him. As the last of the light faded, Bromhead had expected some relief from the heat, but the normal light evening breeze didn't develop and it was as muggy as it had been during the day.

Movement along the trail caught his attention. He turned the binoculars on it. Gilman, leading his three men, ran across the grass. As they entered the village Bromhead stood and waved Gilman over.

"They're on the way, Colonel," he said.

"You saw them?"

"Heard them and then slipped away. Didn't think it was real smart to wait for them to find us. They were moving slowly, as if they had the whole night to get into position."

Bromhead nodded. "I suppose they do. Why don't you take the middle bunker on the north wall as your command post? I'll stay here. Hansen has the one on the south."

Gilman grinned. "This is going to be an interesting twelve hours. The boys in Saigon would be doing flips if they knew what was going on here."

"There's nothing we can do about that." Bromhead stopped as a distant pop drifted to them. It was followed by two others, and then a louder explosion.

"They've hit the mechanical ambush. That puts them about a klick to the east. We can expect incoming anytime now."

"Okay, Nick, get to the bunker. Good luck and I'll see you in the morning."

Gilman stuck out his hand. "Good luck to you Colonel. You're not bad for an officer."

"Thanks." He watched Gilman trot into the dark, disappearing a moment later. Bromhead got up and moved to the rear of the bunker. He stood there for a moment, looking at the jungle across the now burnt grassy plain. He hoped that the listening posts would come in now that the enemy had tripped the mechanical ambush. Then, almost as if answering him, three men appeared at the edge of the jungle. They ran forward, bent low, their weapons in their hands. As they neared the village they slowed, dodged around one of the punji pits and then slid into a bunker.

Bromhead ducked and crawled into his bunker. It was black inside with only a rectangle of gray to mark the firing port. He could hear the rapid breathing of the two men already in there. Their sweat reminded him of the odor of a caged animal. It was the stink of fear that he smelled. Fear from men who hadn't been forced to hold ground in battle. Fear from men who had either had the upper hand at the beginning of the battle or who had fled when the shooting started. Now all they could do was wait for the enemy to attack.

Bromhead moved forward so that he could peer out the firing port. He realized how hot it was in the bunker now. Hotter than the surrounding jungle. Hotter than a steam bath. Hot enough to make his head swim. But he couldn't abandon the position now. The enemy was too close.

From deep in the jungle came a series of pops and Bromhead knew they were firing mortars. That made sense. The first stage of the assault was to fire at the village with mortars. Scare the villagers with the unseen death that rained down on them. But they were prepared and the mortars would do little harm.

Bromhead heard an explosion behind him and then another and another as the shells hit. They tossed up loose dirt and threw out red-hot shrapnel, but the logs covering the bunkers were thick enough to stop the mortars. Even a direct hit would do little damage.

Bromhead crawled closer to the firing port so that his chin was braced on its edge. He watched the jungle, heard the mortars firing, but could not see the flashes of the mortar tubes.

As the shells hit, he ducked, figuring there was no reason to tempt fate. He remembered his first mortar attack. Pure terror, waiting for the shells to fall on him and kill him, or for the red-hot shrapnel to tear into him. He had crouched in the bunker, listening to the retreating explosions of the mortar rounds, never realizing that he was in no danger.

There was a loud bang over his head that shook the bunker. He could smell cordite envelop him and knew that a mortar had hit the logs over him. The man next to him screamed and started to scramble for the entrance. Bromhead grabbed him and held him, saying in French, "Stay here. Stay here." He held tightly as the man fought him as the mortars fell.

And then there was silence. The man stopped struggling, his breathing regular. Bromhead turned back to the firing port, waited, and heard a pop in the jungle.

"More incoming. You won't be hurt if you stay put."

With one hand on the man's shoulder, Bromhead listened to the mortar attack. Explosions all around. Dirt and debris scattered. Shrapnel buried itself in the thick wood of the bunkers. The smell of gunpowder hung in the air. And when they thought it was over, another barrage fell on them.

The longer the attack lasted, the more confident the men became. Bromhead could sense the exuberance in the bunker. He heard the men chattering at one another, chuckling and laughing loudly. A few shouted curses at the VC and the NVA, taunting them. They had realized that the mortars weren't going to kill them.

Then the mortars stopped and at the edge of the jungle, Bromhead could see movement. There were bugles in the distance and shouts in Vietnamese. A whistle sounded shrilly and was answered by another. The leaves at the edge of the jungle seemed to tremble, to vibrate with excitement. Bromhead edged to the side so that his body was protected by the bulk of the bunker logs.

There was a pop overhead and the grassy, ash-covered plain was suddenly bathed in bright light as a flare burst into illumination above him. Bromhead looked over his shoulder, but couldn't see anything. He knew that Gilman was back there somewhere, firing the hand flares, giving the VC and NVA something to think about.

Then there was a burst of fire from a single machine gun and a rising shout. As he glanced out of the firing port he saw the surging charge of the enemy as they ran toward the village.

11

THE MEO VILLAGE

The moonlight silhouetted the enemy as they raced across the ash-covered plain, charging toward the center of the village. In the strange, flickering light caused by the muzzle flashes, the moon, the flares and the fires started by the mortars, the enemy soldiers jerked and fell and died. Bromhead shoved the barrel of his M-1 carbine to the edge of the firing port and began to snipe. He kept his eye away from the sight, aiming by simply pointing the barrel, and then squeezing the trigger.

For Bromhead the battle suddenly narrowed to the tiny sliver that the firing port allowed him to see. A dozen enemy attacking across the open ground, their feet kicking up clouds of ash from the burnt grass.

He emptied his weapon at them, jerked the magazine free and reloaded. He let the bolt slam home and fired again. The enemy soldiers were closer now, no more than fifty yards from him. But more of them were falling and dying. Some were turning to flee as the firing from the bunkers increased.

Suddenly the attack broke and the targets disappeared. Bromhead could hear shouting from the jungle, shouting from the bunkers around him, and moaning from the field in front of him. Through the firing port he saw one of the wounded enemy soldiers trying to get to his feet. He reached for his weapon, fell to his knees and then rose again. He staggered a few feet and collapsed, rolling onto his back.

Moments later the shooting started again. Russian RPD machine guns and AK-47s erupted from the protection of the trees. Bromhead saw emerald tracers streaking into the night. Muzzle flashes winked in the jungle where the enemy hid. He heard the rounds thudding into the logs of his bunker or into the ground in front of the firing port. Dust hung in the air outside, obscuring his vision.

Then in the distance came the sounds of bugle calls, whistles and shouts as another charge came from the trees. Bromhead aimed at the enemy, waiting for them to get closer. Waiting for them to become more than vague shapes. Waiting so that every shot would count.

But the men with him couldn't wait. There was a rippling of sporadic fire as the Meos tried to kill the VC. All along the makeshift bunker line the firing erupted.

But rather than continue their assault, the enemy dived for cover, throwing grenades. At first they fell short, exploding in the open field, geysering dirt and ash that hung in the still, humid night. And then the VC found the range because a few of the grenades began to detonate among the bunkers. A moment later the third volley hit the mark. Dirt and dust choked the men, making it difficult for them to see.

Bromhead shouted at his men and turned to crawl from his bunker. He burst into the clean, night air as a rising shout from a hundred enemy throats cut through the dark. He spun, resting his weapon on the top of the bunker, searching for targets on the dust-choked plain.

Overhead, a flare popped and in the eerie, greenish-yellow light, Bromhead could see clearly. He used the sights of his weapon, firing rapidly. He saw a man clutching at his chest, staggering into the dust and dirt. A second appeared, leaning forward like a man in a high wind. With bayonet extended, he ran toward the American. Bromhead shot him twice and he fell five feet in front of the bunker.

There was a shout from the left as more of the enemy appeared. They charged across the open ground, screaming and shooting. From somewhere on the north came the hammering of a .30-caliber machine gun. Bromhead saw the tracers lancing into the night. Firing increased as the NVA tried to kill the gunner. Grenades detonated near the bunkers, and Bromhead was afraid that the men there would be killed. The noise built slowly until it was a continual roar, washing out all other sound.

Suddenly the firing began to diminish. Bromhead dropped to his knees, crouching behind the bunker. The enemy was now fleeing to the east. As they vanished, there was a volley to his right. On the south, the NVA were launching still another attack.

HANSEN HAD SPENT the mortar attack lying in his bunker, his hands over his ears, praying silently. When the shooting started, he had looked out the firing port but had seen nothing. He fell back to the ground and waited.

Slowly he became aware that the men around him were shooting. The noise from their weapons reverberated in the confines of the bunker. His ears hurt from the pounding and he heard nothing more than the hammering of the M-1s and the machine guns.

He pushed himself forward, shoved his weapon at the gun port, and began to fire. At first he tried to use the sights, but couldn't find a target in the half-light and the rising cloud of dust. Finally he just pointed and shot, pulling the trigger until the bolt locked back.

He reloaded and went through the process again. When his carbine was empty, he moved to the rear of the bunker and crawled out. The enemy was still coming, dodging across the open fields, firing and shouting as they ran.

He reloaded for a third time and opened fire. One of his rounds struck the ground near a VC and he raised the sights. This time he saw the soldier whirl as if slapped in the shoulder. The man lost his weapon, staggered and then fell.

A flare popped overhead, throwing a bright light on the open plain. Hansen could use the sights now. He aimed and fired, knocking down more of the enemy. When he ran out of ammo, he retreated to the second line of defense. He dropped to the ground next to the stilt support of a hootch and reloaded from the cache there.

As he worked with the magazine, he felt the breath rasp in his throat. Sweat made his fingers slippery and he dropped the magazine once. He snatched it from the dirt, wiped it on his sweat soaked shirt, and slammed it into his weapon. He wished he could breathe, or see. Then he wished he was somewhere else.

He wiped the sweat from his forehead with the sleeve of his uniform. He closed his eyes and took a deep breath, ordering himself back into the fight. Ordering himself to kill the enemy, even though all he wanted was to stay right where he was with his head down and his eyes closed. He forced himself to his feet and started back to the bunker line. He was about to open fire again when the enemy turned, running to the east as if to rendezvous on that side of the village.

IN THE NORTH, Gilman was having little luck. After the first assault, he had abandoned the bunker because he found it too confining. He couldn't see the enemy well enough to kill them and if he was going to direct the battle, he had to know where they were.

He dragged the .30-caliber machine gun out and set it on top of the bunker. A group of Meos joined him, taking what cover they could find. When the first of the enemy appeared at the edge of the plain, Gilman shouted, "Wait for them! Wait for them!"

A rippling volley began as the men fired sparingly. A few ruby tracers were greeted by dozens of green. The ground around them erupted and Gilman saw two of his men fall. The rest hung tough, waiting. And then everyone opened fire. A solid wall of lead was thrown out, blowing holes in the on-rushing enemy line. The enemy unit disintegrated until it was no longer an assault but knots of men suddenly fleeing for their lives.

Gilman dropped so that he was seated behind the machine gun. He opened fire, raking the trees two hundred meters away. He inhaled deeply, the odor of the cordite in his nostrils and lungs, acting like a drug. He held the trigger down, lean-ing into the bucking weapon, unaware that he was screaming, ordering the enemy to attack him. Ordering them from the jungle, and ordering them to die.

The shadows that had been prancing inside the trees, or-ganizing the assaults, shouting encouragement to the NVA, forcing the men across the open ground, disappeared in a hail of bullets. Gilman kept firing at them until the belt broke and the barrel of the gun glowed red.

WITH THE SECOND ATTACK beaten back, Bromhead knew that the NVA would try something different. The three-pronged assault had failed because they had spread their men too thin. There hadn't been enough to force their way into the village. Now, in front of him were the scattered bodies of twenty or thirty VC soldiers who had died trying to gain the village. They had barely reached the edge of the bunker line.

Bromhead ran from his bunker, keeping low. He found Gil-man kneeling over the body of a wounded Meo, wrapping a pressure bandage around his shoulder. The man was half sit-ting, half leaning against the logs of the bunker, moaning in pain.

"They're going to hit one side of the village now," said Bromhead quietly.

"Mass their force," agreed Gilman. "Makes sense."

"Thought maybe we should pull everyone out of the bunkers and have them stand by. Shift them around as we need them."

"Better leave one man in each in case the enemy sends a suicide squad. It wouldn't be good to have a dozen VC suddenly appear behind us."

"Then let's get at it," said Bromhead.

Gilman picked up the wounded Meo and carried him to the family bunker only thirty feet away. Inside, Lucas and a couple of the Meo women were working feverishly to bandage the injured. Lucas, still in her safari outfit, was now splattered with blood. As Gilman brought in the wounded Meo, she glanced up but didn't indicate that she saw Bromhead.

Gilman told two of the women to look after the injured man. Before he could get away, Lucas asked, "Will we be able to stop them tonight?"

Gilman shrugged. He rubbed a hand over his face and then wiped the perspiration on the front of his fatigue jacket. "As long as they don't come up with any more surprises, yeah, I think we can stop them."

There was a moan, a quiet, drawn-out sound. Lucas nodded and then went back to her work, shaking out a pressure bandage.

Gilman turned and raced to join Bromhead. Together they moved around the perimeter, giving the villagers instructions. One man was to remain in each bunker, everyone else outside. If the call for help went out, everyone, except the man in the bunker, was to rush to that position.

Then Bromhead returned to the northeast corner of the village to wait. The moon was dropping lower, making it harder to see. There were sounds from the jungle, men moving around, hidden behind the trees. Shots were being fired by both sides, but the sniping was having no effect. Bromhead knew that the big attack was about to be launched. He prayed that it wouldn't be.

He didn't have to wait long. A hundred of the enemy swarmed out of the jungle, funneling toward the corner where he stood. Bromhead slipped to one knee, raised his rifle and said, "Well, shit." He began to shoot. First single, spaced shots, and then as fast as he could pull the trigger. All around him the men did the same until that side of the bunker line was sparkling like a giant Fourth of July display.

The attackers, supported by several machine guns, sprinted forward. Grenades, launched from other weapons, began to walk toward the village. Some of Bromhead's men dived for cover as others broke and ran, fleeing for the safety of the family bunkers. The enemy attack was taking its toll as casualties began to mount. Bromhead knew that his meager force wouldn't be able to turn them this time.

He stood, one hand to the side of his mouth and yelled, "Fall back! Fall back!" But the command was lost in the din of the battle. He turned to run to the south, to alert each position. An explosion on the top of the bunker lifted him and threw him to the ground. He rolled to his back, stunned.

Gilman saw Bromhead fall and raced from his position. He knelt beside Bromhead but before he could speak, the enemy was there. Gilman aimed at two men on the bunker and fired, the muzzle flash reaching out to touch them. One flipped to the ground, rolled over and was still. The other jumped to the right and fired his own rifle. The emerald green tracer burned by Gilman's eyes, momentarily blinding him. On instinct alone, Gilman shot back. His round caught the man in the stomach, dropping him.

Gilman turned back to Bromhead. "Are you badly hurt?"

Bromhead shook his head to clear it. "No. No! Get the men out of here."

Gilman got up and shouted the orders. "Fall back! Fall back!" This time the Meos heard them. They abandoned their positions, running to the rear.

Bromhead struggled to his feet and with Gilman's assistance, raced to the family bunkers. The VC and NVA, seeing part of the defense collapse, surged forward. They leaped the bunkers, ignoring the few men who might still be alive there.

Bromhead grabbed the controls for the claymores. As the enemy materialized in front of him, he hit the firing controls and watched as the mines detonated. Thousands of tiny steel balls slashed through the attackers, tearing them to ribbons. Those who could, turned to flee, running the gauntlet of Meos scattered in the bunkers. Many of the enemy died in the hail of bullets and the crashing of grenades before they could gain the safety of the jungle.

As the attack broke, Bromhead slipped to the ground. There was an overpowering smell of copper in the air and he knew it was the odor of fresh blood. As the firing tapered and then ended except for the periodic sniping of both sides, he could hear the moaning of the wounded and the crying of the women. There was shouting behind him and the children panicked.

"Check the bodies," said Bromhead. "Get the weapons and ammo. They can't be through with us yet."

Gilman relayed the orders in Meo and watched as they quickly swept the field nearby. Once or twice there was a shot as the men killed a wounded enemy. Bromhead didn't like that, but he could understand the emotion. These men had suffered through a mortar attack and two ground assaults. They had seen their friends and members of their families killed. They were not inclined to take prisoners. Each of them knew it was the same thing the Communists would do if the circumstances were reversed. Besides, they had no way of caring for a wounded enemy, no way of guarding him. The safest thing to do was kill him before he had a chance to kill someone else.

As the men took their positions again, Bromhead became worried. They had barely held on during the second attack. It was only the sudden detonation of the claymores that had saved them and he had used the majority of them to break the assault. If the enemy hit them again with an equal force, Bromhead wasn't sure they could survive it.

He crawled forward and checked some of the bodies. He found several dead Meos and began to wonder if the enemy hadn't done more damage than he thought. If the casualties were too high, then another assault would easily overrun the village.

Surrender, he knew, was out of the question. Given the circumstances, he doubted that the Communists would leave anyone alive. They would sweep through the village killing every man, woman and child. They would torture their victims as they killed them. If they hoped to survive the night, they had to fight.

He retreated, circling to the family bunkers. The structures had sustained some superficial damage and a couple of people had been slightly wounded. Hansen had treated them with sterile dressings and then had run back to his post.

Gilman approached, a dozen AKs slung from his shoulders. He leaned sideways and let them slide to the ground. He glanced at the faces of the women and children, seeing masks of terror as they waited for a mortar round to blow them apart or a bullet to slam into them. There were tear streaks on some of the children's faces. Lucas was working hard, bandaging the wounded, passing out water and trying to comfort those who needed it. She ignored Bromhead.

He looked at the pile of weapons lying on the ground, then approached Gilman. "I think we've had it," he whispered. "I can't see how we can beat off another assault."

"Yeah," agreed Gilman grimly. "We've lost too many of our men and used all our tricks. I think it's time to pull out of here."

Bromhead ignored that. Instead he nodded to the rear. "I'll tell Hansen to put out a distress call. Broadcast it in the clear and see if we can't get someone to help us. I'm not sure it'll do any fucking good, but it certainly can't hurt us now."

Bromhead crouched, picked up one of the captured AKs, and worked the bolt, ejecting a live round. He dropped the magazine from the weapon, looked into it and then slammed it home. As he did, a Meo carrying another dozen of the rifles dropped them into the pile.

"If we had the men," said Bromhead, "we could rearm them with these. First time this has happened to me. Plenty of weapons but no one left to use them."

The idea came to him in a flash. He whispered it to Gilman, who laughed out loud. "I don't see why not."

Bromhead spent the next several minutes getting things ready. Once he was sure that Gilman understood, he ran off to meet with the men. Through Beu, he told the men what they had to do. They had to put up a stiff fight at the perimeter and fall back slowly. Draw the enemy in. But for it to work, everyone had to do his part exactly. To falter in the slightest would mean death to everyone. Bromhead, through Beu, made sure they understood.

Bromhead sent everyone to their positions. Next he found Hansen, told him to make the radio calls in the blind, telling whoever might be listening that they were in danger of being overrun. He was to use the emergency frequency of 242.0 because everyone in Southeast Asia monitored that. Once he made the calls, he was to take his position on line. Bromhead then returned to crouch behind the corner bunker and waited.

It didn't take the enemy long to regroup or work up the courage for another assault. There were whistles in the dark. Bugles called to one another and then orders, shouted in Vietnamese, drifted across the open ground. Overhead, a flare burst into brightness with an audible pop. It descended slowly, the burning magnesium describing a smoking arc under the parachute.

As the flare burned out and darkness fell, the VC and NVA swarmed from the trees. There was a rising shout and a burst of firing. Bromhead got to one knee and aimed, returning the enemy fire. Beside him, one of the Meos opened up, cranked off three rounds and then toppled over with a quiet moan, a spreading stain of wetness on his side, looking black in the moonlight.

All around, the Meos began to shoot, their M-1s barking rapidly. The outgoing fire didn't seem to bother the enemy soldiers. They kept coming, their heads down, their weapons at their sides.

Behind them, the jungle was alive with more of them. The Russian-made RPD machine guns raked the Meo positions, kicking up great clouds of dirt and debris, pinning them down. Grenades began to explode. Dust and smoke from the weapons hung in the still night air.

Bromhead got to his feet to meet the onrushing enemy. The firing tapered as the two sides clashed. The fighting changed to hand to hand. Now the air was filled with shouts, grunts of pain, metal clinking against metal. Men screamed insults at one another. A lone man leaped to the top of the bunker in front of Bromhead, who swung his weapon around and pulled the trigger. The enemy was thrown off the bunker.

Bromhead tried to find another target but his own men were so mixed with the enemy that he couldn't shoot for fear of hitting one of his own. He stepped to the rear and an NVA soldier jumped toward him. Bromhead turned, the barrel of his weapon in front of him, but the man swung with his own rifle. The barrels locked and Bromhead's was forced to the side. Bromhead whipped the butt of his M-1 around. There was a solid smack and the enemy staggered. Bromhead kicked upward, his foot smashing into the soldier's crotch. He dropped his rifle, his hands between his legs as he collapsed into the dirt, whimpering.

More of the enemy were rushing from the jungle to join the fight. Bromhead could see that his men were being pushed back. They were giving ground reluctantly, but they were giving it. In minutes it would be too late.

"Fall back!" he ordered. He shouted the command in French and then heard Gilman screaming in Meo. Bromhead saw some of the men trying to break contact, but the VC and NVA were pressing them hard. Some of the men turned and fled, exposing their backs to the VC gunners. A few of them died because of that.

Bromhead kept shouting his order as he retreated. He bumped into the side of the family bunker and stopped. He fell to one knee, aimed and pulled the trigger of his weapon. It recoiled sharply, but Bromhead kept firing until it was empty. With his left hand, he jerked at the pouch on his pistol belt but couldn't get it open.

One of the VC rushed at him. The enemy held his weapon out in front of him, the bayonet extended. Bromhead turned to face the man. As he thrust, Bromhead dodged to the right and used the butt of his rifle. The enemy ducked under it, spun and slashed with the tip of blade. Bromhead parried the swipe, pushing the bayonet to the side. As the man stepped to the left to keep his balance, Bromhead swept his foot in an arc, chopping the VC's feet out from under him.

The soldier fell to his side, landing on his arm. Even over the sounds of the battle around him, Bromhead heard the popping of the bones as they snapped. The VC shrieked. Bromhead kicked again, as if he was trying to put the man's head between the goalposts of a football field, cutting off the screams.

As the enemy died, Bromhead crouched. He began to shout, "Get down! Everyone get down!"

From somewhere near him, Gilman was yelling in the men's native language, giving the same order.

Then suddenly, all around them, AKs opened fire. Nearly a hundred new weapons joined the battle, the green tracers arcing out of the bunker and stabbing into the enemy. The hammering of the individual weapons was lost in the cacophony from the carbines on full automatic.

The attack that had been pressing forward stopped as if it had slammed into a brick wall. There was confusion among the enemy. They faltered.

At that moment Bromhead and the remainder of his men, lying on the ground near the bunker, opened fire again. New weapons added to the fight. Bromhead triggered the last of the claymores and some of his men threw the last of their grenades. The air was split by the explosions. Dirt hung heavy around them and there was the odor of cordite everywhere.

And then the enemy began a retreat. Not a coordinated effort to get out but a headlong flight. Men were throwing away their weapons, running for the safety of the jungle as the village around them erupted into sheets of fire and flame and red-hot steel.

The Meos, led by Gilman, were on their feet, chasing the enemy, forcing them from the confines of the village. At the perimeter, they leaped for cover as RPDs opened up again, their fire raking the ground around the Meos.

As the VC and NVA cleared the field, mortars began to fall once more. In the village, the men scrambled for cover as the enemy weapons exploded around them. Bromhead leaped into a bunker, and felt like shouting. He slapped the men with him on the back, and yelled at them in English. When they failed to pick up on the jubilation in his voice, he switched to French, telling them the fight was over. The NVA were using the mortars to cover their retreat. They had been beaten.

Slowly, from around the perimeter, Bromhead heard the cheering break out as the news spread. Charlie, the NVA, the

Communists had attacked in force and been driven from the field. The villagers, who years before had witnessed the French driven away by the Viet Minh, and who had watched as the Communists forced their will on others, now had beaten the best that the enemy could send against them. Farmers and hunters, trained by French paratroopers over a decade earlier, had avenged the defeat handed them in 1954.

Bromhead, of course, did not know that. He only knew that he had been thrown into the jungle with a stack of supplies and told to assist the Meos. Against almost impossible odds, he had won.

The only thing wrong was the order telling him to collect all the weapons and to get out. He didn't like it, but there was nothing he could do.

As he climbed from the rear of the bunker, listening for the telltale pop of a mortar tube, he was proud of the villagers. They had performed when it was necessary. They had done it well and the bodies of the dead enemy scattered over the field proved they had been deadly.

As the first faint traces of daylight stained the night sky, Gilman left his bunker and walked toward Bromhead. "Well, Colonel," he said, "what next?"

"We get these people organized and get them the hell out of here. The Communists will probably come back with a battalion and anyone they find around here is going to die slowly and horribly."

"How soon?"

"A week, maybe two. Gives everyone a chance to get out," said Bromhead.

"Too bad we can't get a strike company in here to ambush them. Really hit them where it would hurt."

Bromhead nodded. "Let's just be glad we got out of this one alive."

Then, from the distance came the first pop, a noise that could barely be heard over the sounds from the jungle. Bromhead turned and looked over the tops of the trees. There were wisps of fog there, drifting to the south in the light morning breeze. There was a column of black smoke from one of the fires.

As Bromhead watched, specks appeared that slowly turned into helicopters. For a moment he stood and stared, and then remembered that they had just beaten off a Communist attack. If the enemy was close, it would be the perfect time for an attempt to overrun them. He turned to say something to Gilman, but the Marine had disappeared, obviously to set up the security that Bromhead had ignored.

Before the choppers got much closer, Hansen was at his side. "An answer to our radio message."

"You get a call sign?"

"Zulu Six," said Hansen.

Bromhead tore his eyes away from the approaching choppers and laughed. "Zulu Six?"

"You know who it is?"

"Yeah," said Bromhead. "I know who it is. Just like him to arrive on the scene with the help." He glanced at the choppers. "You going to throw smoke?"

Hansen showed him the grenade and said, "All ready. Where do you want them to land?"

"South side of the ville, on that grassy plain. Better advise them of the ash." Just before Hansen ran off, Bromhead added, "This might be the first time in history that the U.S. Cavalry did not arrive in the nick of time."

12

THE AMERICAN
EMBASSY SAIGON, RVN

The conference room was larger and better furnished than the last one Bromhead had been in. The table had enough chairs around it for thirty people, and the majority of them were filled with general officers, admirals, men in dark, three-piece suits, and a couple of colonels. Three chairs had been placed at the head of the table and all were vacant.

Bromhead and his two sergeants, attired in the proper uniforms with all their insignia on them, stood against the far wall, behind a few of the lower-ranking men at the table. Bromhead clutched a green beret in his left hand. He leaned back against the paneled wall and looked at the powder-blue carpeting that seemed nearly a foot thick. Instead of the normal framed prints, there were original watercolors on the walls. Behind the empty chairs were both the American and South Vietnamese flags, although there were no South Vietnamese in the room.

He wondered about the Meo woman that Beu had given to him. She hadn't said a word as the people scattered into the forest after the battle. She had looked at him once and then turned to follow her people. There had never been a real relationship there, but Bromhead felt bad about the situation. He imagined that Beu had taken her back so that she wasn't alone. It was too bad, but there wasn't much that he could do for her.

Gilman leaned close to Bromhead. "How long they going to keep us here?"

"Don't know." Bromhead noticed that several of the men were turning to glare at him.

"Who are these guys?"

"Don't know that, either." Bromhead wiped the sweat from his face. It wasn't that he was hot. In fact, it was chilly in the room, but he was sweating. The summons to the conference had been anything but cordial.

They had been met at the airfield when the helicopter landed. Two MPs armed with M-16s and wearing highly polished helmet liners with a white 716 on them, had been standing at the pad. With them were a Naval captain and an Army colonel. The captain had given Bromhead a sealed envelope that demanded he be at the embassy at nine in the morning, in uniform, to explain what had happened. Neither the captain nor the colonel had been ready when the woman had climbed off the chopper and asked innocently if Bromhead could take her to the hotel.

Bromhead had been thinking about the night at the hotel when the door opened. An Army first lieutenant stepped in and looked at the men at the table. "Gentlemen, the ambassador and General Anderson."

The two men entered. The ambassador smiled and nodded at a couple of the people. "Hello, Fred. Glad to see you."

"Thank you, Mr. Ambassador," said a man in one of the suits.

As the ambassador sat down, Anderson asked, "Are these the three men?"

"Yes, sir," said the lieutenant.

"Okay, Bromhead," said the general, "why don't you let us in on what in the hell you thought you were doing?"

Bromhead moved forward so that he was standing near a corner of the table opposite to the ambassador and the general. He was at a relaxed attention, his hands at his sides, his feet together, and his beret in his left hand. Beads of perspiration stood on his forehead. He knew that anything he said was going to be wrong. These people were pissed and they weren't going to let him forget it.

"General?" he said.

"You were ordered out of the village. You were ordered to recover the weapons. You were not told to engage in combat with representatives of the Laotian government. That was just the sort of incident we were trying to avoid."

"General," said Bromhead. "Mr. Ambassador. My original orders were to train a battalion of strikers to fight a guerrilla action in Laos and to interdict the Ho Chi Minh Trail because of the increased activity on it. That I did."

"Then you did a hell of a job," said the general. "In less than a week you had a combat force and employed them to ambush a column and to defend a village."

"The men were already trained," said Bromhead. "I did what I thought I was supposed to."

"Even after you had been ordered out, you engaged in hostilities with Communists." The general stopped, consulted a folder sitting in front of him, "And you did it all in front of a civilian witness."

"What was I supposed to do? Shoot her? Or let the Communists overrun the village and kill everyone?"

"Bromhead," snapped the general, "I will ask the questions and you'll answer them. And be damned careful because you're about six inches from a general court."

For the next hour Bromhead detailed what happened in the village. Talked about the ambush, the assault on the village and how they had beaten it. Then he talked about the next morning. The bodies strewn over the landscape, most of them Communists.

He talked about picking up the dead Meos and preparing them for transport out of there. How the villagers didn't want to leave the bodies of their dead because of their religious beliefs. He told how Hansen had prepared the wounded for travel with the help of Jane Lucas.

And although he didn't know exactly what Gerber's orders had been, or if he had been operating on his own, he talked about the helicopters landing. With the reinforcements, there had been medics who had treated the injured. Several of the Meos, whose wounds were more serious than the rest, were loaded on the choppers for treatment at the closest Special Forces camp. Arrangements would have to be made to get them back to their families.

The villagers had gotten out of there by noon. Beu had an idea of where they should go. A place they could hide from the Communists. Bromhead had been going to lie about the weapons, but didn't. He told the general that he gave all the captured weapons to the Meos and that he had also given them a number of M-1s and ammunition.

Once the villagers were gone, Bromhead and his men, and Jane Lucas had headed out with the helicopters. They had been ferried to a Special Forces camp and dropped off. Gerber and Fetterman had taken the strike force back to its camp and Bromhead didn't know where they were. Later that day another helicopter had arrived to pick them up. The pilot had no instructions about Lucas since no one had told him about her. Bromhead prevailed, saying that they couldn't leave an American woman on a Special Forces camp. They had an obligation to get her to Saigon where she could get a commercial flight back to the World.

"And that brings us up to date," finished Bromhead.

The ambassador remained silent but the general slammed his hand to the table with a sound like a shot. "You have got to be the dumbest son of a bitch in the United States Army."

"Now hold on, Anderson," said one of the admirals. "I'll admit that some of Captain Bromhead's decisions might be open to question, but I will not tolerate this kind of name-calling, even though he is an Army officer."

For the first time, Bromhead began to relax. It seemed that everything was not as cut and dried as the general was making it seem. A moment later, the admiral confirmed it.

"We are here to determine if Captain Bromhead should be court-martialed. From what I've heard, it would seem that the original scope of the captain's orders was not sufficiently narrowed. His actions seem to be in keeping with those instructions and when they were changed, in midstream, events took control."

"Come on, Peter," said Anderson, "your boy took off on his own, violating his instructions and came up with this cock-and-bull story to cover his ass."

The admiral opened his folder, didn't wait for Anderson to speak. "That is not the impression I get from these reports. At worst, Captain Bromhead could be charged for the cost of some obsolete Second World War weapons that he purposefully left with the natives. Given the fact that the villagers suddenly had possession of a hundred or more AK-47s, I doubt that the M-1s are going to have much of an impact."

That was the way it went for the next hour. The men at the table questioned Bromhead, Gilman and Hansen, touching on all aspects of the mission. The ambassador was surprised to find that no one had known the Lucas woman was in the village until Bromhead and his team walked in. That had been a breakdown in the intelligence system.

The ambassador turned on the CIA representative, demanding to know how that had happened. With all the permits, all the coordination it would take to get her into Laos, the CIA should have known that she was there.

The man simply shrugged. "It's one of those things that slipped through the crack."

The ambassador laughed. "You people want to hang Captain Bromhead and his people and then you tell me that one of the major problems is just something that fell through the crack."

The ambassador leaned over and whispered to the general. He nodded and said, "Lieutenant Davis, would you please escort Captain Bromhead and his men to the waiting room? We'll send for them if we need them again."

As soon as they were out of the room and the door was closed, Bromhead breathed a sigh of relief. "That's got it," he said.

"What do you mean?" asked Gilman. His face was pale; sweat stood on his face and stained the collar of his shirt. Even the underarms of his Class A uniform had been soaked through.

"I mean," said Bromhead, grinning, "that they would have kept us in there if they were going to nail us. They'll fight it out among themselves, trade off and blame each other, but in the end we'll be in the clear. They'll bring us in and pretend that we're in deep shit and had better toe the line, but everyone is going to try very hard to forget this episode."

"You're sure?" asked Hansen.

"Positive," said Bromhead. "I've been through it before. Hell, I was in one deal where they decided to give us medals for it instead of court-martials. I guess that's how heroes are made. They fuck up and someone decides the only way to handle it is hand out a few citations."

It took the men in the conference room two hours to decide what to do. They brought the three men back in, had them stand at attention and the general read them the riot act. Dressed them up and down and told them that for the good of the various services and the U.S. mission in Vietnam, the incident was going to be forgotten. The men were to report to MACV Headquarters in the morning for orders. They were dismissed for the rest of the day.

As they left the room, Bromhead had the urge to whoop, leap in the air and slap the others on the back. With great effort, he walked calmly down the hall until they reached the entrance to the embassy.

Sitting there, dressed in a short skirt and a white blouse, her blond hair washed and combed, was Jane Lucas. When she saw them, she leaped to her feet, at first afraid that it had gone against them, but then realized that they were in the clear.

"What'd they say?" she demanded.

"Chewed us out for getting into the fight with the Communists, but decided that it wasn't our fault. Chewed us out for getting into a fight with an American civilian there but decided it wasn't our fault. Chewed us out for leaving so many of our weapons behind but decided that with all the AKs lying around after the fight, it made no difference."

"Then you're in the clear?" she said.

"Yeah," said Gilman. "In the clear."

Lucas looked at Bromhead. "So what now?"

"Have the day off. Have to report tomorrow. You want to grab some lunch and see if we can waste the afternoon?"

"Lunch is fine," she said, "but let's not waste the afternoon. Let's think of something."

"Sure," said Bromhead.

GLOSSARY

AC—Aircraft commander. The pilot in charge of an aircraft.

ACTUAL—Actual unit commander, as opposed to the radio-telephone operator (RTO) for that unit.

AFVN—Armed Forces radio and television network in Vietnam. Army PFC Pat Sajak was probably the most memorable of AFVN's DJs with his loud and long, "GOOOOOOOOOOD MORNing, Vietnam!" The spinning Wheel of Fortune gives no clues to his whereabouts today.

AIT—Advanced Individual Training.

AK-47—Selective fire assault rifle used by the NVA and VC. It fired the same ammunition as the SKS carbine, which was used early in the war. The AK-47 replaced the SKS.

AO—Area of Operations.

AO DAI—Long dresslike garment, split up the sides and worn over pants. Rarely seen in the countryside.

APC—Armored personnel carrier.

AP ROUNDS—Armor-piercing ammunition.

ARVN—Army of the Republic of Vietnam. A South Vietnamese Army soldier. Sometimes disparagingly called Marvin Arvin.

ASH AND TRASH—Single ship flights by helicopters taking care of a variety of missions, such as, flying cargo, supplies, mail and people among the various small camps in Vietnam, for anyone who needed aviation support.

BAR—.30-caliber Browning Automatic Rifle. A sort of Second World War vintage squad automatic weapon.

BEAUCOUP—Many. Term derived from the French presence in Vietnam prior to the war.

BISCUIT—C-rations. Combat rations.

BLOOPER—See M-79.

BLOWER—See Horn.

BODY COUNT—Number of enemy killed, wounded or captured during an operation. Used by Saigon and Washington as a means of measuring the progress of the war.

BOOM-BOOM—Term used by the Vietnamese prostitutes to sell their product.

BOONDOGGLE—Any military operation that hasn't been completely thought out. An operation or idea that is ridiculous.

BOONIE HAT—Soft cap worn by the grunts in the field when they were not wearing a steel pot.

BURP GUN—Any compact submachine gun, especially the 7.62 x 25 mm Soviet PPSh-41 or any of its variants, such as the Yugoslavian M49 and M49/57, the Hungarian M48 and the Chinese Communist Type 50, which was sometimes called a K-50.

BUSHMASTER—Jungle warfare expert or soldier highly skilled in jungle navigation and combat. Also a large deadly snake not common to Vietnam but mighty tasty.

C AND C—Command and Control aircraft that circled overhead to direct combined air and ground operations.

CARBINE—A shortened rifle for use by cavalry or vehicle crews or special troops, such as, paratroops who require a light, compact weapon. The Soviet SKS and the U.S. M-1 and M-2 are carbines.

CARIBOU—U.S. Army twin-engine cargo transport plane.

CHINOOK—Army Aviation twin-engine helicopter. A CH-47. Also known to the troops as a shit hook. Depending upon the model, it could carry thirty to forty-five troops, or up to eight tons of cargo in an external sling.

CHURCH KEY—Beer-can opener used in the days before pop tops.

CLAYMORE—Antipersonnel mine that fires seven hundred and fifty steel balls with a lethal range of fifty meters. It can either be command detonated by electricity or manually detonated by a trip wire or pull device. It was a directional mine, designed to throw its fragments outward in fanshaped pattern rather than indiscriminately.

CLOSE AIR SUPPORT—Use of airplanes and helicopter gunships to fire on enemy units near friendly troops.

CO—Young unmarried Vietnamese woman. Co is roughly equivalent to Miss.

CO CONG—Female Vietcong soldier.

DAI UY—ARVN rank equivalent to a U.S. captain.

DCI—Director, Central Intelligence. The head of the CIA.

DEAD ZONE—Radio dead spot. A location where, because of the geographic or atmospheric conditions, radio communication is difficult or impossible.

DEROS—Date of Estimated Return from Overseas Service. It came to mean going home.

DING—To shoot someone was to ding him.

DINK—Slang applied initially to any Vietnamese. Later it was used for any person of Southeast Asian extraction; usually it was uncomplimentary.

DINKY DAU—Crazy. From the Vietnamese *Dien cai dau*, literally, off the wall.

DONG—Unit of North Vietnamese money, about equal to a U.S. penny.

E and E—Evasion and Escape.

EOD—Explosive Ordnance Disposal. This aspect of demolitions deals with booby-trapping and the disarming of explosive devices.

FAC—Forward Air Controller. U.S. Air Force pilots who flew tiny O-1 and O-2 light observation aircraft, later OV-10, and directed artillery fires and close air support strikes, served as scouts and as aerial radio relay links and conducted psychological warfare operations.

FAST MOVER—Jet aircraft. Also called oil burners. Usually referred to a tactical support aircraft, such as the F-100 or F-4 fighter bombers.

FCT—Fire Control Tower. An elevated structure protected by sandbags, used within a camp to direct mortar, artillery and machine gun fire when the camp was under attack.

FIFTY—Browning .50-caliber heavy machine gun.

FIIGMO—Fuck It, I've Got My Orders. Pronounced fig-mo.

FIRE ARROW—Large wooden arrow with burning gasoline cans affixed to it used in Special Forces camps to mark the direction of enemy troops for close air support at night.

FIVE—Radio call sign for the executive officer of a unit.

FNG—Fucking New Guy. Any replacement that had recently joined a unit.

FREEDOM BIRD—Name given to any aircraft that took troops out of Vietnam. Usually referred to the commercial jet flights that took men back to the World after they had completed their tour of duty and were eligible to DEROS.

FRENCH FORT—Distinctive, triangular-shaped fortification built by the hundreds throughout Vietnam by the French.

FUBAR—Fucked Up Beyond All Recognition (or repair).

GARAND—Second World War vintage U.S. rifle, .30-caliber M-1. It was replaced in U.S. services by the M-14. The Garand was issued to Vietnamese troops and Special Forces advisors early in the Vietnam War.

GOOK—Derogatory term used by U.S. troops chiefly to describe the Vietcong enemy. Later it was made into a racial slur by the American media, although to grunts it remained a generic term for the enemy without any particular prejudice attached to it, much as calling a German a Jerry during the Second World War. See also Dink.

GO-TO-HELL RAG—Towel or any large cloth worn around the neck by grunts to absorb perspiration, clean their weapons and dry their hands.

GUARD THE RADIO—Term meaning to stand by in the commo bunker and listen for incoming messages.

GUNSHIP—Armed helicopter or cargo plane equipped with miniguns, used in the close air support role.

HE—High-explosive ammunition or bombs.

HOOTCH—Almost any shelter, from temporary to long-term.

HORN—Specific radio communications network in Vietnam that used satellites to rebroadcast messages.

HORSE—See Biscuit.

HOTEL THREE—Helicopter landing area at Saigon's Tan Son Nhut Airport.

HUEY—UH-1 helicopter.

IN-COUNTRY—American troops operating in South Vietnam were all said to be in-country.

INDIAN COUNTRY—Bush slang for enemy-controlled territory.

INTELLIGENCE—Any information about the enemy's operations, including troop movements, weapons' capabilities, biographies of enemy commanders and general information about terrain features in a specific area of operations that would be useful in planning a mission. Also refers to the branch of the military specifically dealing with the gathering and dissemination of such information. Often abbreviated to Intel.

JP-4—Enhanced kerosene fuel used in military jet aircraft and jet turbine helicopters.

KABAR—Generic term for a type of military combat knife.

KEMCHI—Foul-smelling Korean delicacy made of fermented cabbage.

KHMER SEREI—Cambodian underground political group similar to the KKK (which see) but more reliable and trustworthy.

KIA—Killed In Action. Since the U.S. was not engaged in a declared war in Vietnam, the use of the term KIA was not authorized to refer to U.S. troops. Americans were referred to as KHA, or Killed in Hostile Action, while KIA came to mean enemy dead.

KKK—Khmer Kampuchea Kron, a nominally pro-U.S. Cambodian exile group, which operated as guerrillas against the VC in Cambodia. It was often difficult to manage, sometimes being little more than a group of border bandits.

KLICK—One thousand meters. A kilometer.

LBE—Load-Bearing Equipment. Web gear. A pistol belt and attached shoulder harness assembly for carrying a soldier's individual equipment and ammunition.

LBJ—Long Binh Jail. A military stockade near Saigon.

LEGS—Derogatory term for regular infantry soldiers used by airborne qualified troops. Also known as grunts.

LIMA LIMA—Land Line. Refers to telephone communications between two points on the ground.

LLDB—Luc Luong Dac Biet. The South Vietnamese Special Forces. Sometimes disparagingly referred to as the Look Long, Duck Back.

LP—Listening Post. A position outside the perimeter of a camp manned by a few men up to a squad to warn of the approach of enemy troops.

LZ—Landing Zone. An area designated for helicopters to land.

M-1—Either the 8-round, clip-fed Garand M-1 rifle, or the smaller M-1 carbine, which fired low-powered .30-caliber ammunition from a 15- or 30-round magazine.

M-14—Standard rifle of the U.S. Army and Marine Corps during the late 1950s and early 1960s. A replacement for the Garand M-1 rifle, it was itself eventually replaced by the M-16. The M-14 fired the 7.62 x 59 mm NATO cartridge, known to civilians as the .308 Winchester.

M-16—Became the standard infantry weapon of the latter part of the Vietnam War. Derived from the excellent AR-15 assault rifle designed by Eugene Stoner of the Armalite Corporation. The rifle underwent a series of modifications by the U.S. Army, which made it both fire at an excessively high rate and prone to both fouling and jamming. This version, properly known as the M-16A1, is the weapon most grunts carried in Vietnam after late 1966, and accounts for the weapon's poor reputation as a combat rifle. The original AR-15 design was an excellent weapon, and the few examples of it that found their way into Vietnam frequently brought high prices on the Little Black Market in Saigon.

M-79—Short-barreled, shoulder-fired weapon launching a 40 mm grenade. The grenades could be high explosive, white phosphorus or canister (sometimes called buckshot rounds). The M-79 was also known as a blooper, bloop tube and elephant gun, the former deriving from the sound made as the grenade left the barrel, the latter because of the diameter of the weapon's bore. It could effectively launch grenades up to about three hundred and fifty meters, and the bursting radius of the grenades was about fifteen meters.

MACV—Military Assistance Command, Vietnam. The headquarters of the U.S. advisory and assistance effort in Vietnam. MACV (pronounced Mack-Vee) replaced MAAG, the Military Assistance Advisory Group, in 1964.

MARS—Military Affiliate Radio System. A link through Signal Corps and Stateside volunteer amateur radio operators allowing a soldier to send messages to the World.

MEDEVAC—Medical Evacuation. Also called Dustoff. A helicopter used to take the wounded to medical facilities.

MG—Machine gun.

MIA—Missing In Action. Someone who has vanished while in contact with enemy forces.

MOST RICKY TICK—At once. Immediately.

MP—Military Police. They enforced order and escorted convoys.

NCO—Noncommissioned Officer. A noncom. A sergeant.

NCOIC—NCO In Charge. The senior NCO in a unit, detachment or patrol.

NDP—Night Defensive Perimeter (or Position). A secure or defensible position for troops to laager in overnight.

NEXT—The man who said it was his turn next to be rotated home. See Short.

NHA TRANG—SFHQ was located in this city about halfway up the seacoast of South Vietnam. The term was used interchangeably by Special Forces troopers to mean their headquarters.

NINETEEN—Average age of the U.S. combat soldier in Vietnam, as opposed to twenty-six during the Second World War.

NOUC MAM—Foul-smelling fermented fish sauce used by the Vietnamese.

NVA—North Vietnamese Army. Also any soldier of the NVA.

OD—Olive Drab. A dark brownish-green color.

OP—Observation Post. A location for observing the enemy.

OP—Operation. Any military mission.

OPERATION BOOTSTRAP—Program in the U.S. Army to help men on active duty complete a college education. Men in the program were considered to be still on active duty while attending a college.

P-38—U.S. Army designation for a small, two-piece, hinged can opener supplied with C-rations. One of the few really good items of equipment the Army came up with.

PBR—Pabst Blue Ribbon beer.

PETA-PRIME—Black tarlike substance used to hold down dust during the dry season, applied to roads and runways alike. It had a tendency to melt in the extreme heat of day in Vietnam, turning into a sticky black nightmare that clung to boots, clothing and equipment and frequently ruined them. Pilots considered the stuff to be almost useless.

PETER PILOT—Copilot of a helicopter.

PF STRIKERS—Popular Forces. Similar to RFs but used on a more local level.

POL—Petroleum, Oil and Lubricants. Frequently used to indicate a refueling point for aircraft.

POON TANG—See Boom-Boom. The product.

PRC-10—U.S. Army portable radio transceiver used from the Second World War through Vietnam. Eventually replaced by the PRC-25. Both were backpack-type units with a telephonelike handset.

POGUES—Derogatory term used to describe the fat, lazy soldiers who inhabited the rear areas, taking all the best supplies for themselves and leaving the leftovers for the grunts in the field.

PSP—Perforated Steel Plate used instead of concrete paving for runways and roadways.

PULL PITCH—Term used by helicopter pilots that means they are going to take off.

PUNJI STAKE—Sharpened bamboo stake hidden as a booby trap to penetrate the foot. Sometimes dipped in feces or water buffalo urine to increase the likelihood of infection.

QT—Quick Time. It referred originally to the rate of march of foot soldiers, but came to mean talking to someone on the side in order to expedite matters, rather than going through channels.

R AND R—Rest and Relaxation. It came to mean a one- or two-week vacation outside Vietnam, where the soldier was supposed to be able to forget about the war. Shorter, in-country R and R's were also sometimes granted to soldiers who had done a particularly good job. R and R was also known as I and I (Intoxication and Intercourse) by the troops, since these were the two activities most often engaged in when one went on R and R.

RF STRIKERS—Local military forces recruited and employed within a province. Regional Forces were usually used to guard key locations, such as power plants and bridges, and to protect the province political chief.

RINGKNOCKER—Graduate of a military academy, such as West Point. It refers to the ring worn by all graduates.

RON—Remain Overnight.

RP—Rally Point or Rendezvous Point.

RPD—Soviet 7.62 x 39 mm light machine gun.

RTO—Radio Telephone Operator. The radioman of a unit.

RULES OF ENGAGEMENT—Rules that told the American troops when they could shoot and when they couldn't. Full Suppression meant they could fire at will. Normal Rules meant they could return fire only when fired upon first by the enemy. Negative Suppression meant they could not fire back even if fired upon.

SAPPER—Soldier trained in the use of explosives. Especially a VC soldier whose primary job was to blow up bunkers and barbed-wire entanglements during an attack on a camp.

SCRAMBLED EGGS—Distinctive design on the visor of the cap of a Field Grade or General Officer.

SFHQ—Special Forces Headquarters. In Vietnam, SFHQ was located in Nha Trang.

SHIT HOOK—Another name for the CH-47 Chinook helicopter, so called by troops and pilots because of all the "shit" stirred up by the massive rotors during a landing.

SHORT—Term used by everyone in Vietnam to tell all who would listen to him that his tour was almost over.

SHORT-TIMER—GI who had been in Vietnam for approximately the duration of his tour (usually about a year), and who would be DEROSed or rotated back to the World soon. When the Short-timer's DEROS time was the shortest in the unit, that man was said to be "Next."

SIX—Radio call sign for the Unit Commander.

SIX-BY—U.S. Army six-by-six-wheel drive, two-and-a-half ton truck. Also called a deuce and a half.

SIXTY—M-60 General Purpose Machine Gun, caliber 7.62 x 59 mm NATO. Feeding from a disintegrating metal link belt, it had a bipod fixed to the barrel for use as a squad automatic weapon (SAW) and could also be mounted on a tripod, coaxially in a tank turret or on a vehicle pintle mount.

SIXTY—U.S. M-60 Main Battle Tank.

SKS—Soviet-made semiautomatic carbine firing the same round as the AK-47 and eventually replaced by it. It was also used as a generic term to refer to any of the Com-Block or Chicom copies of it.

SMG—Submachine gun.

SOI—Signal Operating Instructions. The booklet that contained the call signs and radio frequencies of the units in Vietnam.

SOP—Standard Operating Procedure.

STEEL POT—Standard U.S. Army helmet used in Vietnam. It consisted of a fiber helmet liner with an outer steel cover.

STRAC—Strategic Army Command or Soldier Trained and Ready Around the Clock.

STORMY WEATHER—Code name for the Cambodian border.

TAI—Ethnic minority group composed of several differing tribes found throughout Southeast Asia and inhabiting chiefly the mountainous regions and the Mekong River delta.

TDY—Temporary Duty.

THREE—Radio call sign of the Operations Officer.

THREE CORPS—Military region around Saigon. Vietnam was divided principally into four corps areas and a few special zones.

TOC—Tactical Operations Center.

TOT—Time On Target or Time Over Target. The former referred to a concentrated artillery bombardment, the latter to the time that an aircraft is supposed to be over a drop zone or bombing target.

TRACK—Any tracked military vehicle. Especially the M-113 APC (Armored Personnel Carrier).

TRUNG SI NHAT—Vietnamese rank equivalent to a U.S. staff sergeant.

TWELVE-SEVEN—The Soviet made Degtyarev 12.7 mm heavy machine gun. Also sometimes called a .51-caliber machine gun.

TWO—Radio call sign of the Intelligence Officer.

TWO-OH-ONE (201) FILE—Military records file listing all the qualifications, training, experience and abilities of a soldier. It was passed from unit to unit so that the new commander would have some idea about the capabilities of an incoming soldier.

UHF—Ultra High Frequency long-range radio. Sometimes referred to as the Uniform, short for its phonetic alphabet abbreviation, Uniform Hotel Fox.

VC—The Vietcong. Often called Victor Charlie (from the phonetic alphabet for the letters) or just Charlie.

VIETCONG—Contraction of Vietnam Cong San (Vietnamese Communist Party, established in 1956).

VNAF—South Vietnamese Air Force.

WIA—Wounded In Action.

WILLIE PETE—Also called WP, Willie Peter or smoke rounds. White phosphorus shells or bombs used for marking targets and as antipersonnel weapons. They were very effective due to their psychological effect.

WORLD—The World. Term used to refer to the United States, where supposedly sanity was still in force, unlike Vietnam, which to the grunts (foot soldiers) was clearly dinky dau. Also sometimes called Stateside, or just the States.

XO—Executive Officer of a unit. The assistant commander.

ZAP—To ding, pop caps at or shoot. To kill someone. Also called grease.

ZIPPO—Slang for a flamethrower, derived from the cigarette lighter popular with the troops. Sometimes refers to a search-and-destroy mission.

Mack Bolan's

by Dick Stivers

Action writhes in the reader's own streets as Able Team's Carl "Ironman" Lyons, Pol Blancanales and Gadgets Schwarz make triple trouble in blazing war. Join Dick Stivers's Able Team as it returns to the United States to become the country's finest tactical neutralization squad in an era of urban terror and unbridled crime.

"Able Team will go anywhere, do anything, in order to complete their mission. Plenty of action! Recommended!"
—*West Coast Review of Books*

AT-1